♦ ♦ ♦ ♦ ♦

Summer Endings

Also by Sollace Hotze:

A CIRCLE UNBROKEN

♦

Sollace Hotze

SUMMER
ENDINGS

♦ ♦ ♦ ♦ ♦ ♦ ♦ ♦ ♦

CLARION BOOKS ♦ NEW YORK

Clarion Books
a Houghton Mifflin Company imprint
215 Park Avenue South, New York, NY 10003

Library of Congress Cataloging-in-Publication Data
Hotze, Sollace.
Summer endings / by Sollace Hotze.
p. cm.
Summary: In the summer of 1945 in Chicago, twelve-year-old Christine anxiously awaits,
along with her mother and sister, news of the political activist father they had to leave behind
when they emigrated from Poland six years before.
ISBN 0-395-56197-3
[1. Immigrants – Fiction.   2. Poles – United States – Fiction.
3. Fathers – Fiction.   4. World War, 1939–1945 – Fiction.]   I. Title.
PZ7.H8114Su   1991
[Fic] – dc20   90-40004
                                                                 CIP
                                                                 AC

BP   10   9   8   7   6   5   4   3   2   1

For Michael, Julie, and David
With love

◆ ◆ ◆ ◆ ◆

Contents

♦ ♦ ♦ ♦ ♦
Summer Endings

1

◆ ◆ ◆ ◆ ◆

A Day to Remember

When news of the German surrender scuttled through the halls of Jane Addams Elementary School on Chicago's North Side, Christine Kosinski closed her ears to the rumors of peace. She couldn't bear to have them not be true. But when the sirens blew at the fire station a block away and a moment later Mr. Brandt, the principal, interrupted classes to announce the news over the public-address system, Christine knew this time the rumors must be true.

"President Truman has announced that earlier today General Alfred Jodl of the German High Command signed the terms of unconditional surrender at Allied headquarters in Reims, France." Mr. Brandt's voice boomed through the loudspeaker. "Although the battle against Japan must continue, children, today is a day to remember. The war in Europe is over!"

At her desk in sixth-grade homeroom, Christine sat with eyes closed and hands folded tightly in her lap. Her breath stopped. She felt a quick stab of pain in her throat. As the other children climbed on their chairs and sailed paper airplanes decorated with swastikas through the air, cheering as they nosedived to the floor, Christine sat motionless and silent. She wanted to hold this moment, taste it on her tongue like a lick of honey lemon, savor it.

The war in Europe is over. Usually she did not like endings, but today was different. *Over* meant an end to a war and the beginning of peace. And how can you have beginnings if there are no endings?

Opening her eyes, she took a deep breath. Thursday, May 7, 1945. A day she would always remember. After almost six years of fighting, the war in Europe had finally ended. Today the Germans had surrendered. Today was her twelfth birthday. Today was special, a magic day, although now that she was twelve, she was too old to believe in magic. Perhaps now Papa would come home. That was the only birthday present she really wanted.

With the shrill ring of the bell at the end of the day, children exploded through the doors onto the concrete playground. Christine put her reading book in her empty lunch box and started the six-block walk home from school alone. Next year she would begin junior high school and ride the streetcar a mile and a half south to school every day instead of walking the six blocks. Usually her best friend Arlene Popelka walked with her. But on Thursdays Arlene took her weekly piano lesson and rode the northbound bus to Broadway.

Most afternoons Christine liked having someone to walk with, but today it was nice being alone. She could think about Papa coming home. She walked slowly, eyes half closed, hearing Mr. Brandt's words play over and over again in her head like one of Rosie's records on their old wind-up Victrola when the needle got stuck. She tasted the words again on her tongue: *The war in Europe is over.* Now Papa would be coming at last.

In the summer of 1939, Papa had been a professor of history and law at the University of Kraków in southern Poland, where he lived with Mama, Christine, and her sister, Rosie. Although Christine had just turned six and was finishing her first year of school, Rosie was already thirteen and seemed very grown-up as she prepared to enter the local grammar school in the fall.

Papa also wrote books on government and world politics, and when the German army invaded the neighboring country of Czechoslovakia in the spring of that year, Papa spoke out against Adolph Hitler. After that, Papa was *polityczny* – political – and it was no longer safe for them to remain in Poland.

Shortly after school let out for the summer holidays, Papa came home one night with train tickets to Danzig in northern Poland on the Baltic Sea, where in two weeks Mama and Rosie and Christine would board a ship for the United States. They had to prepare to leave Kraków in just three days, but Papa could not leave so quickly. He had to stay behind just long enough to sell the house and take care of other business matters. Then he planned to join them in Chicago, where his sister Sophie lived with her husband, Stanislaus.

The last time Christine saw him was at the train station in Kraków on the morning of June 9, 1939.

"Take good care of Roseann and your mama, my little Christine," he had said as he kissed her good-bye. "Remember, you're my good right hand." He hugged her until his mustache tickled her ear. Christine clung to him, wanting never to let go.

As the train steamed slowly out of the station, Papa stood on the platform, waving and smiling as though they were setting off on a long summer holiday by the sea. "I'll see you soon," he promised them. But on September 1, exactly one week before he was to have left Kraków, the Germans marched into Poland and he never came. Since then they hadn't heard from him or anything of his whereabouts. But soon now, Christine was sure, they would have news of him, and perhaps one day he would suddenly appear at their front door, taking them all by surprise. Or perhaps tickets would mysteriously arrive in the mail with a letter telling them to return to Kraków as soon as possible. Rosie wanted to stay in America, but Christine knew Mama wanted to go home.

For the first week of May, the weather was unseasonably warm. A hot summer ahead, the weathermen were predicting. Christine took off her jacket and tied the sleeves around her waist to keep them from dragging on the dusty sidewalk. She turned the corner from Clark Street onto Sheffield Avenue, her street. The trees lining the sidewalk were beginning to show buds, the first hint of the new leaves to come. When she squinted her eyes and looked upward, a faint green haze covered the branches like the layers of pale green tulle on the skirt of Rosie's best dancing dress. Whenever Rosie moved, the tulle whispered like a summer breeze.

Rosie wore Fire and Ice lipstick with nail polish to match, and she wore slacks to work. During the week, she worked the night shift in a factory, packing parachutes. But on Saturday nights she dressed up in her best dress and high-heeled shoes and went dancing at the Aragon Ballroom on Chicago's North Side. The top of the dress was covered with clusters of bright flowers, and whenever she wore it, Rosie looked like a summer garden.

Now that she was twelve, Christine hoped Mama might let her go with Rosie to the ballroom some night.

At the corner of Sheffield Avenue and Addison Street, Christine waved to Mrs. Bertacchi planting her

miniature Victory garden wedged between the Bertacchi's brownstone and Chin's laundry next door.

"Hey, Mrs. Bertacchi!" Christine shouted. "Did you
hear? The Germans surrendered!"

Mrs. Bertacchi glanced up from her garden, her face
alight with a wide smile. "Sure I heard, Christine. It's
been on the radio all afternoon." Mrs. Bertacchi had a
son in the infantry who had been overseas for two
years. She lifted her hands to the sky and laughed out
loud. "Such wonderful news!"

"The war's almost over now, Mrs. Bertacchi. Maybe
you won't need a Victory garden anymore."

Every summer since the war began, Mrs. Bertacchi
had raked up the meager soil and planted vegetables –
head lettuce, pole beans, cucumbers, cauliflower, and
green peas – and every year only a few straggly vegetables survived in the hard clay strip shaded for most of
the day by the two houses.

"It's for the war effort," she always said. "I do what I
can, no matter it is not much."

Christine waved good-bye to Mrs. Bertacchi and
stopped at the curb to wait for the light to change. She
watched the hawkers across the street in front of Wrigley Field shouting their wares. The Cubs were playing
at home today.

"Peanuts, Cracker Jacks!" The vendors' cries echoed
down the block.

"Cold beer here! Ice-cold Meisterbrau! Git yer cold beer right here!"

Christine liked it when the Cubs were at home. The quiet neighborhood came alive with people and noise and the excitement that overflowed the confines of the ballpark into the streets. Today was a perfect day for a ball game. Pennants waved in the breeze, and the mingled odors of hot dogs and roasted peanuts hung in the warm air. Today the flags on top of the stadium pointed to the west. The wind was off the lake, blowing in toward home plate. There wouldn't be many home runs today.

A gull glided in a wide circle above Christine and with a shrill cry swept out again over the lake. Across the street, pigeons and sparrows searched for stray peanuts.

A stooped little man with a hunched shoulder was selling visored caps, blue felt pennants on little sticks, and plastic pinwheels that spun as the wind caught them. He waved to her from the corner. Willy had been selling souvenirs on this corner when she and Mama and Rosie had arrived almost six years ago. He was the first friend Christine had made that summer when she had known no one. Willy had helped her learn to speak English, and sometimes in the summer she helped him sell his souvenirs or watched his stand for him while he slipped over to a bar on Clark Street for a quick beer.

"Hey, Willy," she called through cupped hands, "did you hear? The Germans surrendered!"

"Good news, ain't it, Tina? Ol' Hitler's done for. Soon now your pa will be here for sure." Willy knew everything of importance in Christine's life.

"It's a double-special day, Willy. It's my birthday, too."

A roar exploded from within the walls of Wrigley Field. A second later a ball sailed over the right-field wall, bounced twice on the concrete walkway, rolled across Sheffield, and came to rest in the gutter at Christine's feet.

Instinctively, she stooped to pick it up, and the roar crescendoed, thundering over the walls in a jubilant clamor. In amazement, Christine stared at the ball in her hand. In all of the six years that she had lived across the street from Wrigley Field, this was the first home run she had ever retrieved, and it had landed at her feet like a gift from heaven.

"Willy, look!" she cried, holding up the ball for him to see. "I got a ball! I got a home run!" She danced a little jig on the sidewalk, shouting triumphantly and waving the ball in the air.

"Just for you, Tina. Many happy returns!" Willy called. "Bring it over. Let me see." As Tina ran across the street, the first of the crowd surged from the gates in high spirits, chattering with excitement. What a day it had been! Germany's surrender and a Cubs win, both on her birthday.

Christine dodged the stream of exiting people and ran over to Willy with the ball. He was talking with a man wearing a Cubs cap who had just emerged from the gate. Willy's eyes sparkled.

"Hey, Tina, you know what you done? You caught Phil Cavaretta's home run. It was the run that won the game. The Cubs won this one just for you!"

He was grinning so wide Christine could see the flash of two gold molars in the sun. "Now you gotta get it autographed. Ray here will watch my stand for me, wontcha Ray?" The man in the Cubs cap nodded and moved into Willy's spot beside the stand while Willy took Christine by the hand and marched her through the throngs of people to an unmarked gate halfway around the park.

"Here's where the players come out," he said, "and we're gonna wait right here for old Phil."

Christine rubbed the ball between her hands to convince herself it was real. "Do you really think he'll autograph it for me?"

"Sure he will. All we gotta do is wait." Christine shifted from one foot to the other, too excited to stand still.

Willy was right, and ten minutes later Phil Cavaretta appeared. Christine wouldn't have recognized him out of uniform, but Willy stepped up to him as soon as he emerged.

"Say, Mr. Cavaretta," he said, laying a hand on the ballplayer's sleeve. "This young lady caught your home run. Wouldya be so kind as to autograph it for her?"

Phil Cavaretta smiled at Christine. "You caught my home run? Maybe the Cubs should just sign you up right now."

"Oh, no, sir," Christine said, feeling herself blush. "I didn't exactly catch it. It just sort of rolled right to where I was standing."

"And it's her birthday, " Willy added.

"Sure I'll sign it," Phil Cavaretta said. "I'm real tickled you're the one that got it." He took a pen from his coat pocket and uncapped it. "What's your name, young lady?"

"Christine," she said, handing him the ball. "Christine Kosinski. K-o-s-i-n-s-k-i," she spelled without waiting for him to ask. He wrote something on the ball and handed it back.

"Well, happy birthday, Christina Kosinski," he said. "I guess this has been one helluva good day, hasn't it?"

Christine could only nod wordlessly. Usually she corrected people who called her Christina instead of Christine, but Phil Cavaretta could call her whatever he wished.

"Let me know if you ever catch another," he said with

a wink. "I'll be happy to sign it, too." With a tip of his cap in her direction, he strolled away across the pavement.

Christine walked back to the corner with Willy and waited for the light to change. "I can't believe it," she said, shaking her head and looking up at Willy with shining eyes. "This is the best day of my life. If only Papa was here. If only he could see my ball."

"Well, you just wait a bit," Willy said and gave her a pat on the back. "He'll be here now before you know it."

The light changed. Christine ran across Addison and turned to wave to Willy. He waved back, and they started off in opposite directions, Willy to relieve Ray at his stand and Christine heading toward home.

Above, the sky spread blue and cloudless, stretching over the curved roof of Wrigley Field to the west in a sweep of shimmering light. Christine felt as light as the sky, as light as the breeze that swept the loose tendrils of hair from her forehead. Today was a perfect spring day.

"Whooeeee!" she whooped as happiness rose in her until she thought in another minute it would lose all bounds and she might burst with it. Or fly with it up across the housetops and out over the lake.

"Whooeee!" she shouted as she ran past the Schneiders' fat spaniel sunning on their front stoop. He wagged his tail without raising his head, as though used to such outbursts from this funny girl with the long brown braid swinging down her back.

"Whooeee!" Christine cried again as she arrived at the fourth brownstone from the end, took the six steps in two giant leaps, and landed on the stoop with a great holler of joy. She ran up the three flights to their apartment at the top of the house and collapsed, breathless, on the old plush sofa inside the door.

The apartment was empty. Mama would be at the Aronsons', where she cooked and kept house. And Rosie was almost always out in the afternoons, visiting or shopping with friends until it was time for her to leave for her shift at the factory.

With the living room shades drawn against the afternoon sun, the dim light and silence of the apartment made it feel like church. Christine was afraid too sudden a noise might scatter the feelings inside her like sparrows startled into flight by the raucous cry of a gull.

Perched in the corner of the worn brown sofa that left ridges on the backs of her legs, Christine closed her eyes and tried to picture Papa's face. Lately it seemed that more and more often all she could see was the dark mustache that curled upward above his mouth.

Once, not long after they had come to Chicago, she had dreamed Papa was a sailor. He had rowed in a dinghy all the way from Poland to the shores of Lake Michigan. But just as he was about to land on the beach, a sudden summer squall blew in across the lake. As she watched from the shore, the wind carried him away, eastward across the lake, until he was lost among the gulls swooping above the horizon.

"Papa, Papa!" Christine had called, stretching out her hand to him, but the speck that was his dinghy disappeared behind the oncoming storm. "Papa!" she had cried again, and woke to find herself sitting upright in bed with Mama beside her in the dark holding her close in her arms.

"*Cicho, mala* Christine," she murmured softly. "Hush, little Christine. It is only a *sen*, a dream. *On wkrótce przyjdzie.* Papa will be here soon now."

But as the first year of the war faded into the second, Mama had stopped saying *wkrótce*, soon now, and the little furrow that appeared between her eyebrows grew deeper as first a year and then five years passed. And Papa's face had grown dimmer, until sometimes Christine's memory played tricks and she wasn't sure if the image she saw really was Papa.

She rose from the sofa, tiptoed down the hall leading to her mother's bedroom in the rear of the apartment, and gazed at the photograph of Mama and Papa on Mama's bureau. It was their wedding picture, but it looked like a photograph of a smiling Rosie in white satin and lace standing beside the handsome young man with dark hair who was Papa. A silver filigree frame held the picture in place, the only thing of real value Mama had been able to bring from Poland. Christine stared back at the dark eyes smiling at her from the photo.

Make a birthday wish for me, little Christine, the eyes whispered to her. Squeezing her eyes tight shut, crossing the fingers on both hands, she wished harder than she had ever wished for anything. Slowly, she opened her eyes and smiled back at the young man in the photo. There was no need to tell him what she had wished.

2

♦ ♦ ♦ ♦

The Summer Room

"**P**lease, Mama," Christine begged one warm Saturday night early in June. "Please let me go with Rosie just once, and I promise I won't ask anymore."

"Promises, promises," Mama said with a snort of disbelief. "*Ja znam ciebie za dobrze*. I know you too well, Christine. I let you go once, and forever you will be begging to go again! *Nie, nie*," she said shaking her head.

Whenever Mama was tired or upset or excited, she slipped into speaking Polish. "You are *za mlody*, much too young still, to go to *to miejsce*, that place. Maybe when you are nineteen like Roseann. Maybe then. But not before. Even her I worry about, and one is enough."

That place was the Aragon Ballroom, Rosie's favorite place to go on a Saturday night. It was also the favorite place of the servicemen who overflowed the city during that last summer of the war. Marines on passes from bases in Indiana and Wisconsin and soldiers from Fort Sheridan north of Chicago swarmed along the crowded streets. But mostly the city seemed full of sailors.

They streamed in from the Great Lakes Naval Station on Lake Michigan's waterfront and from the ships anchored at Navy Pier, which jutted into the lake and seemed to float above the gray-green waves like a giant sea turtle. In winter the sailors wore navy blue wool serge under heavy pea coats, but in summer they wore white middies and tight white pants that flared over polished black shoes. Their hair curved back from their foreheads and rippled under white sailor caps that perched like jaunty seagulls on top of the waves.

Every Sunday Christine begged Rosie to tell her about the soldiers and sailors she had danced with the night before, and every so often Rosie even invited one to Sunday dinner. A man's presence in the apartment made it seem strange, as though their little domain of women had suddenly been invaded by something dark and forbidden. Except for Mr. Fazio, who owned the Red Goose shoe store over on Clark Street and who lived on the first floor with his wife and twin baby daughters, their house was inhabited solely by women.

Christine had discovered that Mr. Fazio liked to look up Rosie's skirt whenever she climbed the stairs. When Rosie came in, Mr. Fazio would find some pretext to come out into the downstairs hallway. As soon as Rosie was halfway up the first flight, he would bend over and pretend to tie his shoelace while his eyes slid upward, following the path of Rosie's legs.

Christine wondered why he would want to see up Rosie's skirt when he was married to Mrs. Fazio and must see her naked every night. Sometimes Christine let herself imagine what it would be like to see a man naked, but it was hard because she had never even seen Papa without his underwear. She knew, though, that these thoughts made her no better than Mr. Fazio.

"Rosie," Christine said to her one day after Mama had left for work and Rosie was washing her hair in the kitchen sink. "Mr. Fazio looks up your skirt on the stairs."

"Oh, I know." Rosie laughed and wrapped a towel around her dripping hair. "Poor little man. With a wife like that, who can blame him?" Since the birth of their twins, Mrs. Fazio had grown fat and sat all day reading *Photoplay* and *Silver Screen Magazine*, borrowed from Tillie, who owned the building and had her hairdressing shop in the basement.

"Mr. Fazio's harmless," Rosie said. "It's the men who make a point of *never* looking that you have to watch out for because they keep their interest hidden. They're the ones who don't play games."

"What games are those, Rosie?"

"Don't be so eager. You'll learn soon enough. For now, though, it's enough to know that Mr. Fazio is just playing games. He's not a real threat to anyone," Rosie concluded, and then added with a laugh, "except maybe to Mrs. Fazio."

Christine wished she knew exactly what Rosie meant, but she had decided not to tell Mama about Mr. Fazio. Mama had enough to worry about already.

"*Wkrótce* – soon now," Mama said to Rosie and Christine on a Saturday morning in the middle of June shortly after school had let out for the summer. "Soon we will hear something from Papa. He will contact Aunt Sophie, and we will have news."

Mama's voice sounded cheerful, but Christine knew it worried her that they had never been able to let Papa know where they were living. When they first arrived in Chicago, apartments were scarce, and for several months they had lived with Aunt Sophie and Uncle Stanislaus Nowicki on Milwaukee Avenue. The Nowickis were childless, and Papa was Aunt Sophie's only family. She and Uncle Stanislaus wanted the Kosinskis to live with them until Papa came. But Mama said no, she was very grateful for their help, but three were too many and they must make a home for Papa for the day he would arrive. But by the time they found a place of their own, Poland had been invaded and they never knew if Papa received their letters.

Mama stood in front of the mirror that hung above her dresser and smiled at the reflected image of the three of them together. Since the German surrender over a month ago, her face had brightened and she smiled more often. She smoothed her dress over her hips and lifted a loose strand of hair between her fingers, leaning closer to the mirror to inspect it.

"Roseann, perhaps now you will show me about how you rinse your hair with the juice of a lemon and sit in the sun to make it blonder?"

"Sure, Mama," Rosie said. "And by the time Papa gets here you'll be as blond as Betty Grable and twice as beautiful."

"Betty Grable?" Mama said, smiling at the comparison to the pinup queen of the silver screen. "Really, Roseann? Then maybe I learn to dance, too!" She pulled Rosie by the hand to the kitchen to squeeze some lemons.

Rosie had blonde hair, lighter than Mama's ash-blonde hair that was just beginning to fade into gray. Rosie's hair was like the golden river of milk and honey that flowed to the promised land, Christine thought. No wonder every soldier and sailor in Chicago wanted to go dancing with Rosie. No wonder Mama worried.

"Tell me about the Aragon again, Rosie," Christine begged the following Saturday morning. Mama had left for work, and the two of them were alone in the apartment.

In Kraków they had lived in their own house with a

back yard and an apple tree with a swing, and Mama
had been home every day cooking and sewing and telling stories to Christine while Rosie was at school. But
now Mama worked for the Aronsons, who lived down-
town. Monday through Friday and every other Saturday Mama took the Addison Street bus east to Lake
Shore Drive and transferred south to the Aronsons'
large apartment overlooking Lake Michigan. Sometimes
Rosie urged her to come to work in the parachute factory where Mama could make more money, but Mama
just smiled and shook her head.

"*Nie*," she said, "that work is for younger girls. Besides, Roseann, this work I am used to. You must remember, in Kraków I kept my own house, and very
good if I may say. Now the only difference, is not my
house. But I don't mind. The Aronsons are good
people."

Mr. Aronson was first cello for the Chicago Symphony and often gave Mama free tickets to the concerts.
Sometimes, on a Friday or Saturday night, Mama took
Christine with her. Mama loved music and at home in
Kraków had played Chopin and Liszt on the upright
piano in their dining room. She looked right at home in
the red plush chairs with the little brass numbers that
marked the seats in Orchestra Hall. Somehow it didn't
seem right that now Mama could hear such beautiful
music only by cleaning someone else's apartment.

This Saturday morning Rosie sat at the kitchen table painting her toenails while Mama was at work. Rosie knew Mama didn't approve of red toenails, and she didn't want to worry Mama either.

"Tell me about the Aragon. Please, Rosie," Christine pleaded again.

"Christine, I've already told you a thousand times," Rosie said, dipping the brush in the polish and stroking it on her little toe.

"I know, but sometimes I forget." This wasn't really true because Christine could have described it word for word, but she liked to hear Rosie tell it.

"Well," Rosie said, holding up her left foot and slowly waving it in the air to dry the polish, "it looks like a big garden filled with flowers. Pink paper roses twine around the pillars and look like they're climbing up to the ceiling. Tables with little wire chairs are set around the dance floor if you want to sit. And when the orchestra plays, the lights always dim. . . ."

Rosie paused to inspect her left foot. Satisfied, she switched feet and began to work on her right foot.

"Except . . ." Christine prompted. Rosie was getting to the part she liked best.

"Except?"

"You know, Rosie, the part about the silver sphere – and the stars." She was impatient to hear it.

"Oh, Christine, you've heard this a *thousand* times!"

"Just once more, Rosie. I promise I won't ask any-more."

"Well, right in the middle of the dance floor, hanging from the ceiling, there's a big silver ball, and when the music plays, it slowly turns so the lights reflect into a thousand little prisms of color." She waved her right foot in the air, and her toes looked like five red petals blowing in the breeze. Finished, she screwed the cap on the polish.

"Just like a rainbow," Christine added, imagining the spinning silver ball and the couples twirling under-neath. "Tell me about the ceiling, Rosie."

Rosie groaned.

"Just one last time, Rosie! Please!"

"Well, the ceiling is dark blue and curves overhead like the real sky, and it sparkles with little bits of light. . . ." She paused to pick at a tiny spot of red that had landed on her toe instead of the nail.

"So . . ." Christine prompted again.

"So . . ." Rosie repeated, finished at last with her toe-nails. She looked up at Christine with a smile. "So when you look up, it's like dancing under a shower of stars."

Each time Rosie described it, Christine imagined she was there, dancing with a sailor in a garden bower be-neath the revolving silver sphere and a sky full of twin-kling stars. The sailor looked just like Tyrone Power, her favorite movie actor, with brown eyes that sparkled like the stars in the ceiling and a mouth with soft lips that would bend to hers. This was the most life could offer – to dance with a sailor, to dance cheek to cheek to the music of a big band playing on a warm summer night.

She trailed Rosie out of the kitchen and through the living room to the bedroom they shared in winter. "What makes the stars, Rosie?"

"What stars?" Rosie mumbled from beneath the dress she was slipping over her head.

"The stars in the ceiling."

"Oh, Christine, I don't know." She sighed with impatience and dabbed powder on her nose with a peach-colored powder puff. "Maybe it's lights behind little holes in the ceiling. Maybe it's little bits of mirror or sparkles pasted on – or tiny snips of foil. I don't know."

Rosie sprayed Evening in Paris cologne from an atomizer bottle lightly down the front of her dress. The scent of lily of the valley filled the room.

"Wait till you're older, Christine," she said as she stepped into a pair of open-toed shoes and swung her purse over her shoulder, ready now for a Saturday of shopping. "Wait until you're nineteen. Then you can go yourself and figure it out."

Christine leaned out the open bedroom window that overlooked Sheffield Avenue and waited for Rosie to appear on the stoop. A moment later the front door slammed and Rosie ran down the six steps to the sidewalk. She turned and looked up at the open window.

"What do you want me to bring you today?" she called.

"Bring home a sailor," Christine called back, and Rosie laughed. "And a bag of Bazooka bubble gum," she added.

Rosie nodded and waved. Christine watched until she turned the corner onto Waveland Avenue, then turned back into the room. The fragrance of lily of the valley still hung in the humid air.

An imaginary line divided their room. Each side held an identical twin-sized bed and bureau that Aunt Sophie had given them from her spare bedroom. But Rosie's bed had a spread of pink cabbage roses, while Christine's bed was covered with a tattered Chinese shawl embroidered with dragons she had bought at a rummage sale for a quarter. On Rosie's side of the room was a pale pink easy chair, while Christine's side held a battered wooden student's desk on which she had pasted baseball stickers that now wouldn't peel off.

The room was papered in a print of trellises twined with faded blue morning glories. Except for the paper, the walls on Rosie's half of the room were unadorned, while Christine's walls were hung with eight-by-ten glossy photos of last year's Cubs that Willy had given her at the end of the season. She had strung a length of wire around the molding and hung the pictures from the wire with paper clips. This way she could change their position according to who had the highest batting average.

By the third week of June, the city had already turned hot and humid, and the radio weather reports predicted a scorching summer ahead. The windows in the apartment were open to catch any cooling breeze that blew off the lake. The white muslin curtains in the girls' bedroom puffed inward and then settled limply against the polished oak frame.

Christine sat on her bed and fanned herself with an old copy of *Sporting News* she had borrowed from Willy. She switched on the electric fan on top of Rosie's bureau, turning it to face the spot on the bed where she was sitting. The fan, bent slightly askew and in need of oil, blew warm air in a lazy spiral. But it dried the two little trickles of perspiration that ran alongside her ears. Not even noon yet, and already so hot she felt listless and out of sorts.

Usually by noon on Saturdays Arlene appeared below, shouting from the sidewalk in a voice that Mama said sounded like an air raid siren. "Hey, Tina," she always called in her high-pitched voice, "whatcha-wanna do today?"

Mama said that for someone who had been born in America, Arlene certainly didn't speak very clear English. But Arlene Popelka lived only two blocks away, and she also liked baseball and John Wayne movies. She owned two pairs of roller skates and always let Christine use one.

The Popelkas had a secondhand jukebox down in their basement that didn't need any nickels, and sometimes the two girls danced down there for hours until Mrs. Popelka shooed them outside. Although neither of them knew the dance steps, they improvised, twirling faster and faster, tripping over each other's feet until they ended in a heap on the basement floor and laughed until they ached.

Arlene was a good friend to have, even if she did giggle a lot and run her words together. And on Saturday afternoons, when Mama was at work and Rosie was out, it was nice to have someone to be with.

Waiting for Arlene would be a good time to move, to fix her summer "boudoir," as Rosie jokingly called it. During the winter, they shared the bedroom. But every summer, when the weather grew hot, Christine moved outside onto the little screened-in-porch that hung out over the front of the house. Being on the third floor, their porch was high enough to overlook Wrigley Field, and from it Christine could watch the Cubs games over the right-field wall. This porch was her summer room, a room of her own that no one entered uninvited, a room that offered her a season pass to all the Cubs games, a room where, unobserved, she could watch the world pass by.

Each of the three apartments in the house had one of these small, screened-in porches that jutted out like little boxes from the main part of the house, but they must have been an afterthought because they had no doors. To get out on one, a person had to climb through the living room window.

Carefully, Christine pulled the Cubs' photos from the wire and stacked them in a neat pile in her desk drawer. She carried the wooden desk chair and a small lamp out to the living room and lifted them through the open window. She set the lamp on the chair seat and plugged it into an empty socket on the inside wall below the window, ready for use in the evenings when it grew dark.

She folded the Chinese shawl and stripped the sheets and blanket off the bed. Tugging and pulling until the sweat ran down her face, she hauled the mattress down the hall to the living room. Pausing only to wipe her wet face with her shirttail when the salt sweat ran into her eyes, she managed at last to shove the mattress through the window and out onto the porch.

Returning to the bedroom, she gathered up the pile of bedclothes and the few items adorning her bureau: a blue-enameled comb and brush set Aunt Sophie had given her for Christmas, a wooden music box full of rubber bands that played "Star Dust" when she lifted the lid, and her baseball autographed by Phil Cavaretta. Willy had varnished it with clear shellac so the message wouldn't rub off: *To Christina, my favorite fan. Happy birthday and best wishes, Phil Cavaretta*. She would treasure it always, even with the *a* added to the end of her name.

She arranged the items on the chair that served in the summer as a small bedside table. Making a final trip into the bedroom, she stood in the doorway and looked around. The room, stripped of all her personal belongings, was no longer a room divided, a room that Rosie shared with her. Now it was Rosie's room, filled with the scent of summer flowers, holding no trace of herself.

She gazed at the room, and a strange feeling crept through her toes and up her legs to the pit of her stomach. It was as if some magician had suddenly waved his wand, making her disappear as though she had never existed. Silently she swung the door closed and retreated down the hallway.

Out on the porch she sprawled on the mattress and looked out through the spreading branches of the green ash tree growing from the narrow strip of grass between the sidewalk and the street. The leaves were fully out now, still green and lustrous before the summer dust filtered them gray. She loved this tree even more than the apple tree she had swung from at home in Kraków. The arching branches curved so close to the front of the house that being on the porch was like living in a tree house.

On rainy days, the thick leaves protected the porch

and kept it dry. Usually summer storms blew off the lake toward the back of the house. But now and then a storm blew out of the west, driving great gusts of rain eastward across the rooftops. When the porch became too wet for sleeping, Christine would cover the mattress with a rubber poncho, pull the lamp back inside the window, and spread a sheet on the sofa to sleep until the storm passed.

As she leaned against the cool stone of the house, her thoughts drifted away like bits of fluff from the cotton-wood trees. She felt so peaceful and lazy that she was almost sorry to hear the familiar call from below.

"Hey, Tina! Whatchawanna do today?"

It was Arlene, of course.

3

♦ ♦ ♦ ♦ ♦

Roller Skates

With the coming of peace in Europe, Christine had begun to wait more eagerly for some word from Papa or news from someone who had seen him. Nightly, after Roseann had left for work, she and Mama listened to H. V. Kaltenborn's radio broadcasts, hoping for word about released prisoners of war and refugees arriving from western Europe.

More and more often, though, they were hearing names they soon learned to dread: Auschwitz, Buchenwald, Dachau. As Allied troops moved through Germany and Poland, the scenes the soldiers witnessed were recorded on film. Pictures of emaciated bodies piled in bundles like dry twigs appeared in the magazines and newsreels and wove themselves into Christine's nightmares.

Once in her dreams she saw her father's face pressed against one of the barbed wire fences that held the survivors waiting to be liberated. But just as she was about to reach out and touch him, the face disappeared. She stopped watching the newsreels and planned it so she arrived at the movie theater in time to see only the cartoons and the main feature.

Weekly, Mama checked with the Red Cross, which kept track of each death verified by the discovery of a new body or grave, but the Red Cross had received no word on a Józef Kosinski. They told Mama they would inquire about him among their agencies in Poland and let Mama know the minute they had any word. It was all they could do for the moment, but it was something, and instead of buying a new winter coat that was on sale at Sears, Roebuck, Mama sent a twenty-dollar donation to the Red Cross.

As June ended, war news from the Far East also was hopeful. After three months of fighting, the Japanese had finally surrendered on that little island with the strange name.

"Where's Okinawa, Willy?" Christine asked one Friday afternoon early in July when the Cubs were playing at home.

Christine knew Willy enjoyed company during those long hours in the hot sun. Sometimes, while the game was in progress and business outside the park was slow, they sat together below the right-field wall that by midafternoon shaded the concrete walkway.

"Okinawa's an island in the Pacific," Willy replied.

"Just a speck on the map south of Japan. Nobody never heard of the place till the marines invaded. But it's so close to Japan you could almost spit on it from there. Now, by God, Japan'll be next."

Willy kept close track of what was happening in the war. He had a son named Joey who was a gunner's mate on the battleship *Missouri* somewhere in the South Pacific. Willy was very proud of Joey. Once he showed Christine a picture of him standing on the deck of his ship beside a huge gun turret. In the picture, Joey looked just like one of the sailors Rosie danced with at the Aragon.

"Is Joey's ship near Okinawa?" Christine asked as she watched one of Willy's pinwheels spin lazily in the hot breeze.

"Somewhere near there."

"You must be happy Okinawa surrendered."

"I sure am. But I wouldn't be a bit surprised if Joey's ship didn't head right for Japan."

"Doesn't that worry you?"

"Maybe a bit now and then. But Joey can take care of himself. He's always had luck. I know he'll make it. Just like your pa, Tina," he added after a moment's pause. "One of these days your pa'll come pounding up them stairs and bang on your front door. You wait and see."

Christine always felt better after talking with Willy,

and the next day she was thinking about what he had said as she scrubbed out the old claw-footed bathtub that crouched above the bathroom floor. Mama appeared in the doorway.

"Your little friend Arlene is outside," she announced, "and she's calling for you loud enough to rise up the dead. Hurry go down, Christine, before Mrs. Himmelstein phones up the fire department again."

Mrs. Himmelstein, an elderly widow whose husband had died of a stroke the day Japan bombed Pearl Harbor, lived in the second-floor apartment. She was somewhat hard of hearing. The first time Arlene had come looking for Christine, Mrs. Himmelstein thought someone was shouting that the house was on fire and called the fire department. Then she tucked her Persian cat, Salome, under one arm, picked up the cage that held her canary, Bathsheba, and made her way down the fire escape behind the house.

When Mrs. Himmelstein discovered Arlene sitting on the front stoop still yelling for Christine to come down, she shouted at her in Yiddish and shook her fist until Arlene burst into tears. Sobbing loudly, Arlene started to run home just as the fire truck careened around the corner from Addison Street.

Looking out the front window, Christine saw Arlene sitting on the bottom step of the stoop, roller skates fastened onto her shoes. A second pair sat beside her.

Roller skates meant she had somewhere to go. Arlene never stood if she could sit and never walked if she could ride.

For Arlene, roller-skating was better than walking, especially if she had to go some distance. But lately, since graduating from elementary school, she had decided roller-skating was for children and skated only when it was too far to walk. So today they must be going somewhere out of the neighborhood.

Roller-skating was Christine's favorite thing to do in the summer, especially on a hot day when the faster she skated the cooler the breeze blew. She had never owned a pair of skates, but for her last birthday she had hinted to Mama for a pair of her own.

"Not practical," Mama said. "You are growing too old now for skates. By next year you would have them stuffed in the back of your closet. Skates cost dear. Such money now would be wasted."

So instead of skates Mama had given her a pair of penny loafers that she had also been wanting.

"In junior high you will be liking these better," Mama had said when she handed Christine the package.

But as Christine carefully untied the bow so it could be used again, she could see that Mama looked worried. She pushed back the tissue that covered the loafers, and with a cry of delight, turned to give Mama a big hug.

"Oh, Mama," she exclaimed, "you always get me the

perfect present!" Then Mama had smiled and looked relieved.

Rosie had given Christine her first pair of nylon stockings, which a soldier Rosie knew had been able to buy at the Army PX. So all in all it had been a very fine birthday. But not having a pair of her own skates meant always depending on Arlene.

Looking up, Arlene saw Christine in the window and waved. Her face, as round as the clock above the bleachers across the street, was already crimson from the exertion of skating the three blocks to the Kosinskis' house. Her two blonde pigtails stood stiffly out from behind her ears. Mama always said that the reason Arlene and Christine were such good friends was because they were such opposites.

"Come on down, Tina," Arlene called, standing up and hanging onto the black iron rail of the stoop to keep her balance. "I brought the roller skates."

"Be right down," Christine called back and went to find Mama to tell her she was leaving.

"Arlene's brought the roller skates, Mama," she said to her mother, who was defrosting the refrigerator in the kitchen. "Do you need me to get anything?"

"Just a pound of oleo on your way home, please."

Mama handed Christine a quarter from the chipped sugar bowl on the windowsill above the sink and two stamps from the ration book anchored beneath the bowl.

Christine tucked the money and stamps in her pocket.

"Wait," Mama said as Christine turned to go. "One minute." She poured a sprinkle of cherry Jell-O onto a tray of thawing ice cubes and handed four of them to Christine on two paper napkins. "Take some to Arlene also. I am thinking she will need them on such a hot day, or she will melt like wicked witch in *Wizard of Oz*."

Mama always feared for Arlene's health because her face turned so red in the heat and perspiration rolled down her face in little streams. Christine decided it would be best not to mention Mama's reference to the witch.

"Stop by Mrs. Himmelstein's on your way down," Mama added. "See also what she maybe is needing."

Christine gave Mama a kiss on the cheek and started out the door with her carefully wrapped cherry ice cubes. Rosie always smelled of flowers, but Mama smelled of good kitchen smells: lemon extract, yeast, caraway seed, and cinnamon sugar.

At the second-floor landing, Christine knocked loudly on the door and waited for Mrs. Himmelstein to call her familiar greeting.

"Come. The door is open."

Two and a half years ago Mrs. Himmelstein had slipped on some ice and broken her hip. Now it was difficult for her to walk up and down the stairs, and she seldom left her apartment.

Christine knew what it was like to sit alone in an empty apartment day after day, and often when Mama was at work and Rosie was out, she came down to visit with Mrs. Himmelstein. Mrs. Himmelstein's eyes were growing milky – cataracts, Mama said, shaking her head in sympathy—and her eyesight was failing, so sometimes Christine read poetry to her out of a big book with a soft leather cover decorated with a border of gold fleurs-de-lis. She loved the sound of that word – flur-de-lee – and when Mrs. Himmelstein pronounced it for her and explained that it was the French word for *lily*, it made Christine think of Rosie's Evening in Paris cologne.

Usually she didn't understand the poems that Mrs. Himmelstein liked to hear, sonnets by Shakespeare and odes by a man named Keats, but she liked the way those words sounded, too, and liked the feel of the heavy book in her hands. The pages were of tissue, so thin you could see through them when you held them up to the light, and they rustled softly as they turned.

Christine's favorite poem was the one about the bird, "Ode to a Nightingale," because it sounded so sad, especially the first two lines:

> *My heart aches, and a drowsy numbness pains*
> *My sense, as though of hemlock I had drunk. . . .*

Mrs. Himmelstein had explained that hemlock was the same poison that Socrates, the great Greek philosopher, had drunk when he was forced to commit suicide. That was a sad story. But the saddest story of all was the one Mrs. Himmelstein told her about poor Mr. Keats, who died of tuberculosis when he was only twenty-six. He died in a foreign country, away from his home and all alone except for one loyal friend.

Christine's favorite lines were the ones about the flowers:

> *White hawthorn, and the pastoral eglantine;*
> *Fast-fading violets cover'd up in leaves;*
> *And mid-May's eldest child,*
> *The coming musk-rose, full of dewy wine,*
> *The murmurous haunt of flies on summer eves.*

Reading those lines was like being in a fragrant garden on a summer night.

Sometimes Mrs. Himmelstein told Christine stories about growing up in Austria before Hitler came to power. She and Mr. Himmelstein had lived in Vienna before they emigrated to the United States to escape the Nazi persecution of the Jews.

Before his death, Mr. Himmelstein had played the bass violin with the Chicago Symphony. He was the one who had arranged for Mama to work for the Aronsons, so Mama was very grateful to the Himmelsteins and now in return tried to help out Mrs. Himmelstein however she could.

Cautiously, Christine opened the door, calling out in a loud voice, "It's me, Mrs. Himmelstein!"

"In the music room, Christine," Mrs. Himmelstein called back. Her voice sounded frailer each time Christine visited.

Mrs. Himmelstein called the living room "the parlor" to distinguish it from "the music room," which was actually the second bedroom. In place of the usual bedroom furniture, this spare room was lined with bookcases that overflowed with sheet music, books, and record albums.

A grand piano filled the entire space except for a small love seat against one wall and, next to it, an old radio and Victrola in a cherry-wood cabinet. The radio was hidden somewhere in the bowels of the cabinet, but on top a hinged lid swung upward, revealing a turntable that played records without having to be wound. Christine had never seen another like it.

The curtains were drawn to shut out the sun, and in the dimness of the room it was a moment before Christine saw Mrs. Himmelstein. She sat on the love seat, head cocked to one side like a bird, listening to a string quartet playing on the Victrola.

"Mr. Himmelstein," she whispered, nodding to the record spinning on the turntable. Christine nodded in return and waited in respectful silence for the record to finish playing.

"I'm going shopping, Mrs. Himmelstein," she said as

Mrs. Himmelstein lifted the needle from the record. "Is there anything I can get for you?" The sudden silence made her whisper also.

"What? Speak up, child."

"Shopping, Mrs. Himmelstein," she said in a voice that this time seemed to boom in the tiny room. She pointed to the straw purse that hung over one shoulder.

"Oh, yes. How nice. Could you maybe bring me a half dozen juice oranges and a loaf of pumpernickel?"

Slowly, Mrs. Himmelstein made her way into the dining room, took two dollars out of an envelope buried beneath a pile of table linen in the oak sideboard, and handed them to Christine. Stuffing them into her pocket, Christine edged toward the front door. The ice cubes were beginning to drip through the paper napkins.

"A glass of lemonade before you go, dear? So hot it is today, not fit for man nor beast."

"No, thank you, Mrs. Himmelstein. Maybe next time. Arlene is waiting for me downstairs."

"Oh, yes. I heard her. Your little friend who shouts 'fire!'" Mrs. Himmelstein said, nodding. She had never quite forgiven Arlene for causing her to make that undignified trip down the fire escape. "Just the oranges and the bread then, dear."

The door started to swing closed when suddenly Mrs. Himmelstein's head appeared again. "And perhaps the laundry you left last week at Mr. Chin's?" she called as Christine started down the steps. "So nice of you that would be."

"What took you so long?" Arlene grumbled as Christine appeared on the stoop.

Without bothering to explain, Christine handed her one of the ice cube packets that was by now dripping sweet cherry water onto the sidewalk. Gratefully, Arlene sucked on the remains and then patted her red face with the wet paper towel.

"You'll make your face sticky," Christine said, sucking on her own ice cubes. "All the flies will want to lick it." She laughed out loud at the picture in her head of Arlene racing down the sidewalk followed by a swarm of flies, all trying to light on her face.

"Yuk. That's disgusting," Arlene said with a grimace. She wadded up the paper towel and threw it into one of the garbage cans that sat beneath the stoop. "Besides, it's too hot today even for flies."

"Where are we going?" Christine asked as she sat on the bottom step to fasten the skates. She fitted the toe of one shoe into the metal brackets and then tightened them with the key that hung on the string Arlene handed her.

"Mom wants me to buy flowers for Oompah's grave," Arlene said. "She can't go because Bennie's got the measles." Bennie was Arlene's little brother, with whom they spent as little time as possible. Oompah was the Popelkas' grandfather, who had lived with them for as long as Christine had known them. Last summer he had died of double pneumonia.

Oompah had given piggyback rides and treated the girls to Good Humors. Once, the summer after the Kosinskis had moved to Chicago, he had treated Christine and Arlene to chocolate ice cream sodas. With the straw boater he always wore in summer set squarely on his head, he marched them the few blocks north to Peavy's Drugstore and boosted them onto the stools in front of the soda fountain.

Christine had never tasted an ice cream soda, but she had seen pictures of them that looked delicious, with foam running over the sides of the glass in little sudsy rivers. When her soda arrived, she had leaned over and sucked deeply on the straw.

The fizz bit into her throat and stung her nose. It made her cough and her eyes water. She didn't want to drink any more, but she also didn't want to be impolite and hurt Oompah's feelings by telling him the soda hurt her throat. Taking a deep breath and holding it, she sucked on the straw until the glass was empty of the chocolate fizz water and she could eat the ice cream sitting in a lump in the bottom.

Oompah had always made her feel like she was his granddaughter, too. When he died, Mama went with her to his funeral. During the service, Christine had tried hard not to cry because it might not have seemed right for her to cry for someone else's grandfather. She didn't want the Popelkas to think she was presumptuous. But later that night, lying in her bed on the porch, looking up past the rooftops at the stars spread across a field of purple velvet, she had thought about Oompah alone in his grave and Papa alone somewhere in Poland. And she had cried softly into her pillow for Oompah and for Papa, who were both alone.

It was a year ago today that Oompah had died.

"Mom wants us to put some flowers on his grave," Arlene repeated as she skated out onto the sidewalk. "I have money for the flowers, and she said we could each have a dime for a cherry Coke."

"Okay," was all Christine said in reply, but secretly she was pleased. It would be nice to visit Oompah's grave and take him some flowers. And it meant skating a long way.

Christine tightened the second skate, hung the string with the key around her neck, and skated down the sidewalk to the corner, where she turned to wait for Arlene.

"Last one down the block's a monkey's uncle," she called as they started across the street.

"It's too hot to race!" Arlene protested, puffing to keep abreast of Christine.

In a sudden surge of goodwill, Christine slowed her pace to match Arlene's. There was no hurry. They had all day.

Today they would skate uptown all the way to Saint

Boniface Cemetery, much farther than they usually went. And the cemetery was only two blocks west of the Aragon Ballroom. Maybe, if she was lucky, she could persuade Arlene to go with her to the Aragon. Maybe, just maybe, they would be able to look inside.

As they skated together down the sidewalk, slowing only to avoid bumping people unlucky enough to be walking, Christine's toes tingled and little icicles traveled up the backs of her legs. In spite of the heat, a shiver of anticipation crept along her spine. There was no doubt about it. She could feel it in her bones. Today was going to be an adventure.

4

♦ ♦ ♦ ♦ ♦

Setting Out

Arms swinging, legs churning, the two girls skated up Sheridan Road to Irving Park.

As they waited for the light to change, Arlene tugged on Christine's arm.

"I'm hot. I need a drink," she said. "Let's stop at Peavy's Drugstore now." She wiped her perspiring face on her shirtsleeve and bent over to unfasten her skates.

"Wouldn't you rather have it later?" Christine asked as the light changed and they started across the street. "We're not even halfway."

"I mean just for some ice water. Mr. Peavy won't mind. We'll stop back for Cokes on the way home."

With a sigh, Christine stepped up on the curb and bent to unfasten the leather strap around her ankle and tug off her skates. Going anywhere with Arlene on a hot day meant many stops. She didn't like asking for free ice water, but Arlene never seemed to mind. Her red face was a convincing argument, and no one ever turned her down.

Carrying their skates, the girls opened the door and were met by the jangle of a bell and a puff of cooler air. Christine stopped in the entryway to admire the window display advertising Chen Yu *Mandarin Red* lipstick and nail polish. It looked like an ad in one of Tillie's movie magazines.

Christine gazed in admiration at the larger-than-life-sized cardboard cutout of a woman with long, flowing black hair and a long, flowing red satin negligee. The woman was lying on a white bearskin rug. One hand rested gracefully on top of the bear's head. Her fingers were long and tapered, and each nail had been lacquered a bright crimson that matched the negligee. The woman gazed out at the busy Chicago street with one sultry dark eye. She looked just like Rosie in a black wig.

With a lingering gaze, Christine turned away from the woman in the window to follow Arlene into the store. The thermometer bolted outside the door read ninety-six degrees. Inside the door, another thermometer showed eighty-four. The drugstore was dim. Mr. Peavy always kept the lights off during the day in summer. Two big fans on pedestals at either end of the store moved the air back and forth so that customers always felt a breeze.

As Christine stepped across the threshold, Mr. Peavy's voice called from behind the high prescription counter at the back, "Don't stand there with the door open. You're letting the heat in!"

Hurriedly, Christine closed the door and turned to Arlene, who was peering into the dim interior.

"Oh, boy!" Arlene said in a loud whisper. "Look, Tina. Peter Horner is working today." She giggled as she pointed to a boy polishing glasses behind the soda fountain. "Isn't he just about the cutest thing you ever saw?"

Christine peered over Arlene's shoulder. The boy behind the counter looked like Tyrone Power, the movie star, with his wavy brown hair and very white teeth. Peter Horner was good-looking, not cute. Cute was for boys their own age, and this boy was clearly much older. Probably at least sixteen.

Christine slid onto the stool beside Arlene at one end of the counter. A man and woman sat together at one of the little round, wire-legged tables Mr. Peavy had set up in the center of the store. At the other end of the counter, two teenaged girls leaned across the marble counter, conversing with Peter Horner.

One of the girls laughed at everything he said, and the other one was leaning so far forward that her halter top billowed out, revealing a pale half-moon where the line of her suntan met the white skin of her breast. Christine quickly looked away as Peter sauntered down the length of the counter and stood in front of them. He must have been able to see right down to the girl's waist.

"What would you two girls like?" he asked with a smile. Close up, his teeth looked even whiter. His eyes were hazel with little flecks of yellow that made them look alight. He was even better-looking than Tyrone Power.

"Hi, Peter, what's new?" Arlene said with a giggle. Christine kicked at her ankle. "Ow," Arlene complained. She turned and made a face at Christine.

"We'll just have some ice water, please," Christine said in a small voice, and she cleared her throat.

Peter stared at her, a puzzled look puckering his forehead. Then he smiled with a look of sudden recognition. "Say, aren't you Roseann Kosinski's kid sister?"

"Yes," Christine replied, embarrassed at having been singled out for his attention. "How did you know?"

"She's Christine Kosinski," Arlene broke in with a haughty tone. "Do you know Rose Ann?" She pronounced the name in two distinct syllables as though it were two separate names.

Christine looked at her with surprise and almost laughed. It was the first time she had ever heard Arlene call Rosie by her formal name.

Peter filled two glasses with ice and held them under the water spigot until they overflowed.

"Anybody who's got eyes knows Roseann," he said, grinning at Christine as he set the two glasses in front of them. Christine could feel herself blushing and looked down at her glass of water.

"Actually," he continued after a moment, "it's my older brother Jerry who knows Roseann. But I've seen you with her. Jerry was in her class in high school. They dated some. I had a real crush on her then."

He wiped a ring of water on the counter with a cloth. "Of course, I was only fourteen then," he added quickly and moved toward the other end of the counter, where the two girls were still watching him.

The girl in the halter top, with a quick glance down the counter, leaned forward and whispered something to Peter. They both laughed. Christine was sure it must have been some joke about her and Arlene. She could feel her face flush.

"Come on, Arlene," she said spinning her stool in the opposite direction and sliding off. "Let's get going. We can't hang out here all day."

"Maybe not," Arlene said with a giggle in Peter's direction. "But I'd like to!"

Outside the door, Christine stopped short. "I left my skates," she said and headed back into the drugstore. As she retrieved them from under the counter, she was careful not to look at the three still laughing together at the other end. As she started out the second time, Peter suddenly called to her.

"Say hello to Roseann for me, will you, Christine? Tell her Jerry Horner's brother says hello."

"Sure," Christine mumbled, careful not to look at him on her way to the door. Her mouth felt full of cotton wads like the dentist used, but at the door she suddenly turned and blurted, "Thank you for the ice water."

"No problem. Anytime," Peter said. Christine thought she had probably never seen such a sparkling smile, like an ad for Pepsodent toothpaste.

"Don't put on your skates," Arlene said as Christine came out. "There's a flower shop a half block down Irving Park, near Graceland Cemetery. I'll buy the flowers there."

"How do you know Peter?" Christine asked as they crossed to the north side of Irving Park.

"Isn't he really the cutest boy you ever saw?" Arlene went on before Christine had a chance to comment. "Actually, it's my brother Jim who knows him. Peter's in his class. He comes over sometimes."

"You're lucky to have an older brother."

"Ha! A brother can be a real pain in the neck. I think you're lucky to have an older sister. You can borrow her clothes."

The thought of wearing Rosie's clothes made Christine laugh. She would look like a little girl playing dress-up. Besides, Rosie was much too particular about her clothes to loan them.

Arlene didn't know how lucky she was. She had not just one but *two* brothers. She had had a grandfather who had lived with the family for many years and an-other grandfather who was still alive and lived in Bloomington, only a few hours away. And, most im-portant, she had a father who came home every night, a father who sat in his morris chair and read the *Daily News* and smoked his pipe.

Christine loved the aroma of pipe tobacco. Papa had smoked a pipe. Every night he had sat in his chair and read the paper aloud to Christine on his lap while she snuggled in the crook of his arm. Now, except for Willy and Uncle Stanislaus, there was nothing but women in her life. Not a single man. Mr. Fazio didn't count.

"Here," Arlene said, pointing to the entryway of a small shop whose window was shaded against the mid-day sun by a faded green-and-white-striped awning.

Entering the shop was like walking into a garden in full bloom. Christine had never seen so many flowers, not even at Oompah's funeral. Vases of red and pink roses and dark green ferns filled the space behind two glass doors, and pots of gold and amber chrysanthe-mums clustered in one corner.

Remembering Mr. Peavy's warning about letting in the heat, Christine stepped across the threshold and pulled the door closed behind her. A little bell jangled above the door frame and summoned the proprietor from behind a curtain at the back of the shop. Arlene approached her with a businesslike step, but Christine hung back. Deep purple and magenta flowers that she didn't recognize exuded a sweet, musky scent that made her think of the dark-haired woman in Mr. Peavy's window.

Buckets on the floor full of long-stemmed gladioluses and snapdragons caught her eye. She leaned over to pinch one of the little blossoms, making the "dragon" snap. Then she moved to the counter to join Arlene, who was counting out five one-dollar bills to the woman behind the counter. The woman's nose was blue-veined and beaked, and as she handed back the single quarter, her nostrils quivered.

"This is for the way home," Arlene said, pocketing the quarter. "Look what I got for Oompah's grave." She pointed to the flowers she had picked out. The bouquet was mostly daisies enlivened by a few pink gladioluses and snapdragons and one red rose on a very long stem.

"The daisies were the cheapest," Arlene whispered, "but I think they look okay with the others."

"Are you taking them to Graceland Cemetery?" the woman asked as she gathered them up.

"No, we're going to Saint Boniface Cemetery," Arlene replied.

"Oh my. That's quite a distance on such a hot day. We wouldn't want the flowers to wilt, would we?" The woman frowned as she considered this problem. Then her face cleared. "I'll just wrap some wet newspaper around them first to keep them from drying out," she said with a smile. She took a page of yesterday's newspaper and soaked it in the sink at the back of the store. Then she wrapped the wet newsprint around the stems and covered it all in a cone of green waxed paper.

"There you are, dear," she said, handing the somewhat damp package to Arlene. "That should keep the flowers fresh until you get there. But carry them carefully."

Outside, the early afternoon heat rose from the sidewalk, a wall of hot air that met the girls head-on as they left the shaded shop. The smells of the city – exhaust, dusty concrete, and unemptied trash bins – swept away the last vestige of the sweet perfume of the flower shop.

"Let's cut through Graceland," Arlene said as they fastened on their roller skates again. "It'll be shorter. Cooler, too. At least it's shady." Already her face had turned red, and perspiration dotted the bridge of her nose.

"What about the ghosts?" Christine asked. She knew Arlene was nervous about ghosts and wouldn't even go near a cemetery on Halloween. Skating to Saint Boniface was one thing. Arlene was going there for a special reason. But skating the long block through the center of Graceland was something else again. She was surprised Arlene would even suggest it.

"Oh, that's no big deal in the middle of the afternoon," Arlene said with bravado. "Ghosts only come out at night or during storms." She paused to glance at the cloudless sky. "So there won't be any problem with ghosts today. The only problem may be the caretaker. He doesn't like kids cutting through. My brother Jim says he's mean."

Christine gave a dubious glance toward the cemetery. Then with a shrug of her shoulders, she said, "We might as well. But let's keep a close eye out."

The two girls skated west to the corner of Clark and Irving Park. At the entranceway, they paused for a moment. Then, hand in hand, they swung open the black wrought iron gate and skated into the cemetery.

5

♦ ♦ ♦ ♦ ♦

A Brief Encounter

oday even the cemetery was hot, although shaded areas offered some relief from the sun. Christine was glad they had come. She liked cemeteries. They were always so peaceful and quiet. As she skated beside Arlene along the walk that bisected the cemetery from Irving Park to Montrose Avenue, she was aware of the street sounds gradually fading behind them, growing fainter as they neared the center of the cemetery midway between the two main thoroughfares.

The cemetery itself was silent, as though they had left the city far behind and had traveled to some distant countryside. Rows of gravestones marked the orderly progression of the dead, shaded by great old elms and maples that protected their silent charges from rain and sun alike with widespread branches stretching above the quiet paths. Christine liked to read the inscriptions on the graves. Sometimes she imagined the person who was buried in a certain grave and what kind of life the person had led.

Some of the inscriptions were strange, some funny, some sad. The saddest ones were for the babies and young children whose dates of birth and death showed that only a few years or months or sometimes just a few days were all that a child was given. Christine often wondered what had happened to these children. She liked the gravestones that explained the death, like the small oval stone at the edge of the path that read:

> *Mary Alice Wiggins*
> *Beloved Daughter Whose Short But Precious Life*
> *Was Ended by Diphtheria*
> *1889–1891*
> *Blessed Are the Pure in Heart*

Ahead and to the right stood a tall, ornately carved monument with freshly turned dirt around its base.

"Look," she said to Arlene and pointed. "It's brand-new. Let's see who it is."

They stopped in front of the monument to read the inscription engraved on a polished brass plate set into the stone.

"'Henry Wadsworth Ryerson,'" Arlene read aloud. "'Born January 12, 1875. Died July 1, 1945.' Gee. He died just ten days ago."

"I wonder who he was? He must have been very rich."

"He sure has a fancy stone. But look. Not a single flower. Poor guy." Arlene pulled a daisy from the cone of wrapped flowers and laid it beneath the carved stone. "That should make him feel better," she said with satisfaction.

Christine stared at the newly turned earth and the fresh white daisy against the black dirt. The image of Papa lying buried in some newly dug grave surfaced in her thoughts. An icy finger crept down her spine. For the first time since they had left Poland, the idea that Papa might not be alive became real to her. She thought of Oompah lying in the casket, his thin hands folded on his chest as though he were deep in thought. Papa couldn't look like that. Somehow she would know if Papa wasn't still alive somewhere. She turned away from the grave to look down the long walk stretching ahead and wished now they had never come here.

"Let's keep going." She tugged on Arlene's arm.

Arlene looked at her with concern. "What's wrong, Tina?"

"That grave makes me think of Papa." Christine blinked back the tears.

"Gosh, Tina, don't think about that. This guy's got nothing to do with your father. Look how old he was." Arlene pointed to the engraving on the brass plate, doing a quick calculation on her fingers. "He was seventy. That's old, almost as old as Oompah was."

In silence they skated side by side down the path, but a moment later Arlene suddenly turned off the concrete, stepped onto the grass, and sat down in the shade of a row of hydrangea bushes in full bloom.

"I have a pebble in my shoe," Arlene explained as she laid her bundle of flowers in the grass under the bush and loosened her right skate. "It's killing my little toe."

While Arlene pulled off her brown oxford and white anklet and shook out the offending pebble, Christine lay back in the grass and glanced up at the small patches of blue sky. Through the canopy of green leaves filtering the light, the sky looked like pieces of the jigsaw puzzle that Mrs. Himmelstein had kept on her card table before her eyesight began to fail. Arlene was right. That man Henry Ryerson had nothing to do with Papa. She had been silly to even think about it.

"It sure is peaceful here," she said in a soft voice to let Arlene know everything was all right now, and at the same time to avoid disturbing any ghosts who might be sleeping there.

"It sure is." Arlene pulled on her skate and tightened the clamp. "I always forget how big the cemetery is until I have to – " She stopped in midsentence, cocked her head to one side, and held up one finger.

"Ssshhh! Something's over there!" Arlene pointed toward the row of bushes.

Christine thought Arlene was just being nervous about ghosts and started to reassure her, but Arlene silenced her by holding her raised finger to her lips. "Sshhhh," she whispered again. "Maybe it's a German spy."

Christine wanted to remind her that the Germans had surrendered and wouldn't need a spy in Graceland Cemetery, but she heeded Arlene's warning finger and remained silent.

On hands and knees, Arlene crept forward to peer between the bare slender trunks of the hydrangea bushes. She turned briefly to motion to Christine, her blue eyes narrowed to a squint, her fingers pressed against her mouth to suppress a giggle.

"Look," she whispered, pointing again through the bushes.

Holding her feet apart to keep her skates from clanging, Christine crawled beside Arlene and peeked through the clump of bushes.

A short distance beyond, on a patch of grass beside a gravel path, she saw a couple on a blanket. It was a marine and a woman in a blue flowered print dress, lying side by side. On the far edge of the blanket their shoes sat together in two neat pairs. The man's arm lay across the woman's shoulders in an embrace. They were kissing.

Christine could see that the marine's eyes were closed, just like in the movies. The woman was on her side, facing away from the row of bushes. Her skirt was pulled up around her thighs, and Christine saw the marine's other hand curved around one of her legs, his fingers stroking the flesh just above the knee as he continued to kiss her.

Christine wondered how it would feel to be kissed like that. A strange tingle pricked at the base of her scalp.

"Boy, they're really making out!" Arlene said in a loud whisper.

"Sshhh," Christine hissed in warning, afraid the couple might hear.

Christine knew they shouldn't be watching. This wasn't a movie, this was different. Movie actors knew they were being watched, and that made it okay. But these people didn't know. This was meant to be private.

"We better go," she whispered to Arlene and turned around to leave. A man was standing behind them on the concrete path, glowering. Before she could stop herself, Christine gave a half-stifled cry.

The man stood, legs apart, feet in heavy boots planted firmly on the concrete walk. His left hand gripped a rake. His right hand, curled into a tight fist, was thrust against his hip. Christine wondered where he had come from and how long he had been standing silently behind them.

"Oh, my gosh," she heard Arlene say in a soft croak beside her.

Speechless, Christine stared at the man's angry face. She wondered if he might attack them with the rake and started to stand up but forgot she was wearing skates. Her feet rolled out from under her, and she sat back down with a spine-jarring thump.

The man glared through narrowed eyes, his thin lips turned down in a sneer. His gray hair was dusty, his creased face streaked with sweat marks that ran down in little paths like snails' trails. Even at a distance Christine could smell the acrid odor of sweat, the heavy sweat of a man who has been working all day in the hot sun.

"Let's get out of here," Arlene said in a muffled voice. She clambered up and held out a hand to help Christine to her feet.

"Not so fast, you two." The man's voice was a growl. "What do you two think you're doin', anyhow? You ain't supposed to be roller-skating in here."

He walked toward them, his eyes lifting to gaze across the top of the hydrangea bushes. Then his eyes snapped open and his lips parted in a lopsided look of disbelief.

"Hey, you two!" he shouted across the top of the bushes. Christine heard a woman's high-pitched voice cry out, but her words were inaudible. "Whadda you think you're doing in here? This here's a cemetery for the dead, not some lovers' lane."

From beyond the hedge came the murmur of a man's voice and then hurried footsteps down the gravel path, away from the hydrangea bushes.

"So that's what you two was up to," the man said, facing the girls. "Just a couple of Peeping Toms. Ain't you two a little young for that?" He took another step toward them.

Christine's stomach lurched. Was he going to try to grab them? If he came any closer, she would yell for help. But now there was no one to hear her.

"We weren't doing anything," Arlene said defiantly, but her voice was strangely high.

"Oh, you weren't, huh? I seen what you was looking at. Out for a cheap thrill, huh?"

"We weren't looking at anything," Arlene protested.

Christine looked at her out of the corner of her eye. Arlene knew that wasn't true. The man was right. They were nothing but Peeping Toms.

"You don't expect me to believe that, do you?" the man said. "If that's what you little twerps want, you better watch out. You might just get more than you bargained for."

His right hand came away from his hip and moved to the top of his worn trousers. Christine raised her eyes to the man's face and saw that he was looking right at her, a knowing grin stretched across his face.

He had found her out, had seen into the darkness hidden inside her, had read the secret desires she had not even dared to put into thoughts. She took a step backward away from this man who could see inside her.

The last thing she noticed was that his teeth were crooked and stained brown from tobacco. Then anger pushed away the fear.

"Come on," she said in a loud voice and grabbed Arlene's hand. She lunged away from the man, across the grass to the walk. Arms flailing, the two girls skated as fast as they could go down the stretch of concrete toward the exit on Montrose Avenue.

Behind them they could hear the man calling after them, his voice a bellow in the still afternoon. "I seen you, you little twerps, you Peeping Toms! And I better not ever see you in here again!"

"This way!" Arlene veered to the right on a diagonal path.

Ahead, the far corner of the cemetery suddenly appeared.

"Is he coming after us?" Arlene asked with a gasp as they rolled toward the brick wall.

Christine turned to take a quick look behind them. The path was empty. No one was in sight.

"No," she said and heaved a sigh of relief. "He's not there."

A moment later the girls arrived at the corner of the wall where it met the thick hedge bordering the cemetery on the east side. Panting and perspiring, they pushed through the narrow opening to the safety of the sidewalk beyond.

6

♦ ♦ ♦ ♦ ♦

A Bouquet of Flowers

The two girls leaned against the wall to catch their breath. Arlene was panting. Her red face dripped with perspiration.

"Yuk," she said, wrinkling up her nose. "Wasn't that man awful? I told you he was mean." She looked down at her empty hands. "Oh, my gosh!" she yelled. "I forgot the flowers! That stupid man made me leave Oompah's flowers." Her eyes filled with sudden tears.

Christine put her arm around Arlene's shoulders to comfort her, feeling the loss herself. They had gone through so much on such a hot day, and now Oompah wouldn't even have his flowers. "We could go back and get them," she suggested tentatively.

"Not on your life! I'm not going back in there with that creep." Arlene turned from the gate, and Christine gave a small sigh of relief. Arlene wiped her wet face with her shirttail. "I guess we might as well go on home."

Slowly they skated east on Montrose toward Sheridan Road.

"Mom's going to kill me," Arlene said after a moment in a quavering voice, and Christine knew she was close to tears.

"We still have the quarter," she reminded Arlene in an effort to cheer her up. "We can stop at Peavy's on our way home." She glanced sideways at Arlene. "Maybe Peter will still be there."

"Yeah, I could use a Coke," Arlene said, her face brightening. "Let's go."

The afternoon sun baked the sidewalks. The cloud of heat that rose to envelop them in a suffocating blanket was almost visible. Christine's shirt was wet with perspiration and clung to her back.

By the time they reached Peavy's Drugstore, Arlene's face was crimson, and even Christine was thankful to step into the shade of the doorway. As they entered the store, they held out their arms to catch the breeze from the fans. But as she closed the door behind them, Christine could see that Peter Horner had been replaced by a skinny girl with buck teeth and acne.

"Hell's bells!" Arlene muttered, copying her mother's favorite expression of dismay. Her scowl revealed her disappointment. "This is really my lucky day! Instead of Peter, we get old horse-tooth." She slid onto a stool with a grunt of disgust.

A little knot of disappointment settled in the center of Christine's rib cage. She, too, had been looking forward to seeing Peter again.

"Hi, Arlene, what can I getcha?" the bucktoothed girl said in greeting. Belatedly Christine recognized Cathy O'Hoolihan, who lived across Halsted from the Popelkas.

"Cherry Coke," Arlene said in a desultory voice.

"Nickel or dime?"

"Dime. And lotsa ice."

"Same for me," Christine said.

"I can give you the Cokes," Cathy said. "But we're all outta ice."

Arlene groaned and rolled her eyes to indicate that this was the final straw.

"It's the heat," Cathy continued as she poured a dollop of cherry syrup into two glasses and then filled them from the spigot behind the counter marked Coca-Cola. "Everybody's been wanting lotsa ice."

In silence the two girls slowly drank their warm Cokes, taking small sucks on their straws, delaying the moment when they would have to leave the drugstore, fasten on their skates, and make their way the four long blocks to Christine's house.

When they had both noisily inhaled the last drops

from the bottoms of their glasses, Arlene dug into her pocket and plunked the remaining quarter onto the smooth marble counter.

"Keep the change," she said airily to Cathy as the two girls slid off the stools and started for the door to fasten on their skates for the fourth time that day.

When they glided to a stop in front of her stoop, Christine sat on the bottom step to remove the skates. "Thanks for letting me use them," she said as she handed them to Arlene. "See you next week."

From the stoop she watched Arlene, shoulders drooping, slowly roll away down the block toward Addison.

"Hey, Arlene," she called. Arlene turned back to face her. "I'm really sorry about the flowers. Maybe your mom won't be too mad."

Arlene gave a flicker of a smile. "Maybe," she said and started down the sidewalk a little faster, shoulders a little straighter.

As Christine started up the stairs, the door to the first-floor apartment suddenly opened and Mr. Fazio stepped out.

"Oh, it's you, Christine," he said, and his flat voice revealed his disappointment. "How's it going?" Without waiting for a reply, he turned and reentered the apartment. Christine made a face at his retreating back.

Halfway to the second landing, she suddenly stopped, left foot poised on the step above. The errands for Mama and Mrs. Himmelstein – she had forgotten them entirely. Now she would have to go back out. Her legs ached; her armpits itched with prickly heat. Maybe she could tell Mama the A&P was out of oleo. Maybe Mrs. Himmelstein had forgotten all about the oranges and pumpernickel. No, she wouldn't have. With a sigh of resignation, Christine turned and started back down the stairs.

She walked down Waverland Avenue toward Clark Street, her feet dragging, her throat dry and scratchy with the dust from the pavement. Somehow today hadn't turned out the way she had expected. Everything had gone wrong. Oompah's flowers lay beneath the hydrangea bushes, wasted, left there to wilt and die in the grass at Graceland Cemetery. She and Arlene had never reached Saint Boniface, so of course there had been no reason to stroll past the Aragon Ballroom. If this had been a lucky day, perhaps they might have been allowed to look inside.

It was the man in the cemetery who had made everything go wrong. She should tell Mama. But Arlene was probably right – he was just trying to scare them. Mama had enough to worry about, and, besides, Mama would ask her questions, would ask why she had been watching the couple on the blanket. She knew she could not answer because then Mama might see inside her, might see what the man had seen.

At the A&P on Clark Street, Christine collected a

pound of oleo, six juice oranges, and a loaf of pumpernickel. She put Mama's change in her left pocket, Mrs. Himmelstein's change in her right pocket.

Outside the store, she headed southeast on Clark Street toward Sheffield. By the time she arrived at Chin's laundry, her arms ached as well as her legs.

Inside the shop, clouds of steam rose in the air and tickled her dry throat, making her cough. It must have been 110 degrees in the store, but Mr. Chin stood unperturbed behind the counter, arms folded against his chest, his shiny face the only sign of discomfort.

"How ah you, Chlissie?" he said with a wide grin of welcome. "Not seen you all this week."

"Hi, Mr. Chin." Christine smiled in return despite her aching arms and legs. Mr. Chin was the only one who called her Chrissie instead of Tina. She liked to hear the way he said it, with *l*s instead of *r*s. Like Willy, Mr. Chin's smiling face always made her feel better.

Everyone in the neighborhood knew the Chins were Chinese, and early in the war Mr. Chin had painted *CHINESE* across his window in big red letters above the word *Laundry*. But every now and then some group of hooligans from outside the neighborhood would harass him, soap his window, or call him a dirty yellow Jap.

Once on Halloween someone strung a dead black cat over his door. Christine had helped him wash the soap off the windows and had even offered to help him bury the cat in the backyard in one of the boxes he used for clean laundry. They had been good friends ever since.

"You mama not have some laundry for one, maybe two weeks, Chlissie."

"I'm here for Mrs. Himmelstein's laundry, Mr. Chin." She took the remaining dollar bill out of her right pocket and laid it on the counter.

Mr. Chin handed her a package of laundry wrapped in brown paper. "Dollar even," he said.

"I hope Mrs. Chin is feeling okay," Christine said as she turned toward the door. "Say hello to her for me."

Usually Mrs. Chin worked behind the counter or at a sewing machine in the back of the shop where she stitched splitting seams or sewed on loose buttons. But she was expecting a baby, and she stayed in their apartment above the shop, away from the heat of the steaming water, the irons perched on top of scorched ironing boards, and the hot mangle Mr. Chin used for sheets and flatwork.

"She fine," Mr. Chin said. "Baby come any day now."

He walked around to the front of the counter and opened the door for her. With her groceries in one arm and the laundry in the other, Christine trudged the block home.

At Mrs. Himmelstein's, Christine could hear her through the door talking in a loud voice on the telephone. She let herself in, set the groceries and the laundry and the change on the dining room table, and waved a good-bye to Mrs. Himmelstein.

"Thank you, thank you, dear child," Mrs. Himmelstein called loudly into the receiver and waved back. Usually she offered Christine a cup of hot tea, but today Christine was thankful Mrs. Himmelstein was preoccupied. Just the thought of hot tea made her prickly heat itch.

Upstairs, Christine found Mama in the kitchen preparing supper.

"Rosie is out tonight. Tonight is just the two of us," Mama said with a smile. "In a few minutes now it will be ready, but we will be needing the oleo for our bread."

Christine took the pound of oleo out of the grocery sack and put the pale white mound in a bowl. She broke the little gelatin capsule of yellow dye over the white margarine and began to knead it like a lump of yeast dough, over and down. She loved the feel of the cool margarine as it softened and oozed between her fingers. She loved watching it change from white to butter yellow, and making the oleo look like butter made it taste better. She put the finished margarine into a covered glass dish and set it on the table.

Tonight it was especially nice to have Mama home. After supper, the two of them sat together in the living room and listened to the radio while Mama darned stockings. They didn't talk much, but it was comforting to know Mama was there.

After the late news, Mama turned off the radio and put away her mending.

"Good night, *malutka*, little one," she said to Christine, giving her a hug. "*Slotkich snów*. Sweet dreams."

"Good night, Mama." Christine pressed her cheek against Mama's. It felt cool and soft and smelled of lavender.

After preparing for bed, Christine turned out the lights, leaving one lamp lit in the living room for Rosie. Then she climbed through the window out onto the porch.

Lying on the porch at night was the best time of all. During the day, the streets below were busy with people coming and going, but at night the streets were quiet, almost deserted except for an occasional couple strolling in the darkness.

Stretched out on her mattress, Christine turned her face to catch a whiff of breeze from the lake. She listened to the rumbling and clanging of the Howard Street El a block away and thought of all the unknown people moving in and out of those cars, the unseen faces all with places to go. She wondered if she would ever join them.

As she drifted toward sleep, a jumble of faces floated through her head like balloons floating in space. First Papa, blowing smoke rings from his favorite pipe. Then Oompah in his straw boater marching beside Willy in his Cubs cap. And finally Mr. Chin, his round smiling face like the Cheshire cat in *Alice in Wonderland*.

As she drifted deeper toward sleep, one last image forced its way into the dark space behind her eyes – the caretaker in the cemetery. His features were lost in the shadows, so it was not his face she saw but his hands. They were holding a bouquet of wilted and dying flowers. The drooping blossoms seemed to beckon to Christine, drawing her forward as they nodded in the breeze.

She drifted deeper into the dream until she was at the Aragon Ballroom, standing in a bower of long-stemmed red roses. The orchestra was playing, and as the music swirled around her the lights dimmed, and she was alone in the middle of the dance floor. She looked up, but the stars in the ceiling were drifting away, fading into the black night sky.

A short time later she awakened to the beat of rain strumming the roof tiles above her head. Through half-closed eyes, she saw the rain slanting westward across the cone of light cast by the lamp on the street corner. The lake breeze and rain had cooled the city, bringing relief from the heat and washing the dusty streets.

She pulled the sheet tighter under her chin. In the darkness, tucked in the safe nest of her mattress, she lay motionless and listened to the sound of wind and rain dancing together to soft music in the background. The music drifted through the half-open window from the living room, the melody of "Sunrise Serenade."

In a haze of sleep, Christine raised herself on one elbow until she could peer over the edge of the windowsill. The lid of the old Victrola was raised, and a record
was spinning on the turntable. Farther back in the
shadows, beyond the bright rim of light cast by the
lamp, Rosie was dancing with a sailor. She was wearing her favorite dress with the green tulle skirt and flowered top.

The worn rag rug had been rolled aside. Slowly, in
time to the music, Rosie and the sailor turned together
on the bare floor, dancing cheek to cheek. As the sailor
spun her across the floor, his hand pressed against her
waist. He dipped, bending Rosie backward over his
arm in a graceful arc until her hair fell in a cascade of
gold against the pale green of her skirt.

Then, slowly, slowly, he pulled her upright until
they were again dancing cheek against cheek. The sail-
or's fingers seemed to weave among the profusion of
flowers on Rosie's dress.

Under the cover of darkness, Christine watched the
dancing couple until the song ended and Rosie lifted the
needle to turn the record. She thought of the marine
and the woman lying together, of watching them from
behind the screen of hydrangea bushes. She remembered his arm flung across the woman's back, the hand
on her flesh, and for a brief moment she tried to imagine
that she was the woman. But then the caretaker's face,

grinning at her in their moment of shared discovery, pushed the image away.

Slowly, Christine sank back to her mattress and closed her eyes. As the notes of a new song drifted through the window, Christine gave a soft sigh and waited for the music to lull her back to sleep.

7

◆ ◆ ◆ ◆ ◆

Box Seats

On an overcast Saturday afternoon at the end of July, Christine was sitting on her porch watching a Cubs game across the street when Arlene turned the corner at the end of the block. She came down the sidewalk at an uneven gait, first dragging her feet, then bounding ahead in short leaps as she concentrated on bouncing a little rubber ball on a wooden paddle.

Before Arlene could shout her usual greeting, Christine called down to her in a loud whisper. "Come on up. The door's open. But don't make any noise. Rosie's still asleep."

If awakened too soon, Rosie was apt to be out of sorts and take it out on Arlene. When Arlene wasn't around, Rosie called her "your fat friend with the loud voice."

Earlier in the day, after Mama had left for work, Christine had pulled one of the dining room chairs through the window and now sat propped on top of the chair back, her own back supported by the stone wall of the house. From here she had a perfect view of the ball game over the right-field wall. Beside her on the windowsill sat a half-eaten sandwich and a glass of lemonade, a little on the tart side because of the shortage of sugar, but refreshing all the same on a sultry day.

Christine could feel the excitement beginning to rise around Wrigley Field with the steam from the hot dog stands. The Cubs were in first place. In past summers hopes of a pennant had dangled in front of them for a brief time. But always the hopes had faded by midseason when potential home runs became just long fly balls, batting averages slumped, and pitchers threw everywhere except over the plate.

But not this year. This summer was different. August was about to begin, and the Cubs' batters were still hitting, the pitchers still throwing strikes. The baseball season was moving into its final two months with the Cubs clinging stubbornly to first place.

The crowds flocking to the games each day were bigger, noisier. Every day the stands filled a little earlier, and the ticket vendors hung STANDING ROOM ONLY signs in their little windows almost as soon as they opened for business in the morning. By game time, the rooftops overlooking Waveland and Sheffield were lined with men, and on Sundays the rooftops were so full that

Christine feared everyone might fall through to the apartments below.

Sometimes on Sundays Mr. Fazio asked Tillie for permission to invite his friends to sit on the rooftop because it was her house, but often during the week the roof was filled with Tillie's own friends. From her perch, Christine could hear them now, walking above with heavy steps. Their voices bounced off the flat roof and carried below.

She settled back to watch the game. The Cubs were leading one to zero. Stan Hack was batting in the bottom of the second inning. After fouling off the first pitch, he connected with a fast ball, and a sudden roar rose from Wrigley Field. The ball sailed over the fence onto Sheffield Avenue, and shouts echoed from the rooftops along the street. On the roof above, men's feet stamped their approval.

In the window beside the porch, the shade suddenly snapped open and Rosie's scowling face appeared at the same moment Arlene stepped through the window onto the porch. For a moment Rosie glared at Arlene, then her face disappeared back into the bedroom.

"Oh, boy," Arlene said with regret. "Now I'm on Rosie's blacklist." She plunked down on the empty chair.

Behind them the girls could hear Rosie's bedroom door open with a bang.

"I guess Rosie's up for the day," Christine said with resignation. "She wishes the Cubs were in last place. Then nobody would bother coming to the games." Christine rolled her eyes at this evidence of disloyalty.

Arlene glanced across the street to the houses on Waveland. "Well, you've got the best seat of all – a nice shaded porch. I wish I lived here." She paused a moment. "And you can get something to eat whenever you want it," she added in a hopeful voice.

"You want a sandwich? Let's go fix it while they're between innings."

The two girls climbed back through the window and headed for the kitchen.

Christine spread peanut butter on one slice of bread, grape jelly on the other, and then clapped the two together. Purple jelly oozed from the edges onto the worn linoleum counter. Christine lifted the sandwich gingerly onto a plate and handed it to Arlene just as Rosie swung through the door, barely missing Arlene.

"I'm going to the matinee," she said to Christine, giving Arlene a disdainful look. "I wish Tillie would keep all those men off our roof. A girl can't sleep around here anymore with all this baseball craziness."

She held out a dark brown eyebrow pencil to Christine. "Here," she said, "put my seams on for me, will you? I can't get them straight."

Although the skin on Rosie's arms and face was pale, her legs looked darkly tanned and smooth as though she

were wearing stockings. But nylons were in short supply because of the war, and Christine knew Rosie's
stockings came from a bottle of leg makeup. She tried it
once herself when Rosie was out, but her legs had
turned splotchy and streaked with dark orange marks.

Kneeling on the floor, she took the eyebrow pencil
and drew a straight line that started midway up Rosie's
thigh, a few inches above her hemline, and ran all the
way down her calf to the heel of her shoe. Then she
drew a duplicate line on the other leg, providing Rosie
with two seams for her stockings.

"You're a pal," Rosie said, giving Christine a hug and
heading back through the door. After a breezy wave of
her hand, the door swung closed and Rosie was gone.

Arlene gazed after her with rapt admiration. "Gee,
do you suppose I'll ever look like that?" she asked wist-
fully.

"No," Christine replied matter-of-factly. "You won't,
and neither will I. Let's go watch the game."

Back out on the porch, the two girls leaned their
chairs against the brick wall to watch the game and eat
their lunch.

"Boy, this is the life," Arlene said thickly, her mouth
full of peanut butter. "All the comforts of home and a
good place to watch the ball game, too."

Christine nodded contentedly. "I bet any one of those
men up there would gladly trade places with us."

"Sure, I bet they'd pay good money for these seats."

Arlene's chair came down with a sudden thud that almost knocked over Christine's lemonade. "Wow! What a great idea, Tina. We could *sell* these seats and make lotsa money. By the end of the season, we'd be rich!" Her round face glowed with excitement.

"I don't know," Christine replied dubiously. "Do you really think they'd *pay?*"

"Sure. For nice seats behind a screen and out of the sun? You bet they would."

"But how would we sell them? Who would come?"

"We'll advertise. Make signs and sell tickets along Sheffield and Waveland. I betcha the men who sit up on the roofs would buy 'em. The games are always sold out now, even the bleachers. Lotsa men would like our seats."

Christine thought this over in silence. Arlene was right. Why would anybody want to bake in the sun on a rooftop when he could sit on a nice shaded porch? She turned to look through the window. Eight chairs stood around the dining room table. She measured the porch with her eye.

"You know," Christine said slowly, still calculating, "if we leaned my mattress up against the wall, we could fit all those chairs out here. We could have two rows of four chairs. How much would we charge?"

"Well, we'd have to keep it reasonable. Maybe a quarter a seat?"

"That sounds kind of high."

Arlene thought a moment. "Well, then, how about twenty cents for the front row because they're the best seats and fifteen cents for the back."

Christine counted quickly on her fingers, using her left hand for the back row, her right hand for the front row.

"That would be a dollar forty for every game," she said with mounting excitement. "And there are at least twenty-five more home games." This time she reached for a pencil and piece of scratch paper and did a careful calculation.

She looked up in amazement. "Wow! That means by the end of the season we could have thirty-five dollars. We really would be rich."

Thirty-five dollars. It was more money than she had ever dreamed of having. Why, with only her half she could almost buy Mama that new coat for Christmas and maybe even a new bottle of Evening in Paris for Rosie.

Arlene's eyes gleamed. "Wow," she echoed. Her eyes fell on the remains of their sandwiches and Christine's half-empty glass of lemonade. "And we could make sandwiches and sell them. And lemonade. Men always get hungry and thirsty at ball games."

As the idea grew, so did Christine's excitement. "Of course, we can't sell beer, but we could let them bring their own if they wanted." A sudden thought hit her. "But not on weekends," she added, sobered by the notion of Mama watching men carrying beer into her home.

"Okay," Arlene agreed. "Just weekday games."

"And only people we know," Christine added as an afterthought.

"Yeah, we sure don't want any loonies like that guy in the cemetery!"

"The Cubs go on the road next week, so that gives us plenty of time to get it all ready," Christine said. "And Monday we'll make the posters and the tickets."

Overcome for the moment by a vision of riches, Christine settled back into her chair to watch the Cubs move one game closer to the National League pennant, a miracle neither she nor Willy had ever dreamed of last April.

8

♦ ♦ ♦ ♦ ♦

Great Expectations

As anxious as she was for Monday to come so that she and Arlene could begin preparing for their business venture, Christine looked forward to Sunday because Uncle Stanislaus and Aunt Sophie Nowicki were coming to dinner. On alternate Sundays, she and Mama and Rosie took the bus across town to Milwaukee Avenue and were treated to dinner at the restaurant Uncle Stanislaus owned and operated with Aunt Sophie's help.

But even when it was the Nowickis' turn to come to the Kosinskis', Uncle Stanislaus always brought a special treat, sometimes from the restaurant but often something he had fixed himself at home. This Sunday he brought homemade root beer and strudel made from cherries he had picked off the tree in their backyard.

"How's my favorite princess this fine day?" he

greeted Christine and set his parcels on the hall table to
free his arms for a hug. He didn't look at all the way
Christine thought the owner of a restaurant should
look. He was a slight man, thin and wiry, and very dap-
per. He always wore a vest and a gray fedora, even on
the hottest days, and never seemed to perspire.

Behind him, Aunt Sophie puffed up the stairs, sweat-
ing profusely after the three flights but ready with a
smile by the time she reached the door. Aunt Sophie,
plump and large-boned, stood taller than Uncle Stanislaus by two inches. She liked to joke that she could boss
him around, and they called each other Stan and Ollie
after the comedy team of Laurel and Hardy.

Christine liked Uncle Stanislaus not only because he
always brought them treats but also because he called
her princess and told her she was the real beauty of the
family.

But Aunt Sophie was Christine's favorite because she
was Papa's sister and Christine could talk to her about
Papa without worrying her.

"Your father got all the looks in our family," she often
said with a hearty laugh and a poke at Uncle Stanislaus's
ribs, "but I got the free meal ticket!"

Mama always prepared something special on Sundays when the Nowickis came to dinner. This Sunday
she fixed spareribs and sauerkraut, Uncle Stanilaus's favorite. She had been saving ration stamps for two weeks
to buy the meat. After dinner they sat around the din-

ing room table playing hearts and drinking root beer. The day passed so quickly that Christine didn't have time to think about the plans for Monday.

But the following day she heaved a sigh of relief when Rosie prepared to leave the apartment early in the afternoon,

"There's no point in trying to sleep past noon when the Cubs are in town," Rosie stated in disgust as she headed out the door. "Nothing but noisy men stomping and yelling on the roof."

As the door slammed behind her, Christine gave a little whistle. Somehow she knew their plans would be much easier to carry out with Rosie out of the apartment.

While she waited for Arlene to arrive, Christine climbed out on her porch to enjoy the shade of the green ash tree and wait for the game to begin. From where she sat she could see men already gathering on the rooftops along Waveland. They carried folding chairs and coolers for their beer.

Above the fourth brownstone diagonally across the street stood a giant billboard with a picture of two soldiers talking at a bar while behind them hovered a Japanese woman with very slanted eyes and elephant ears. In the lower right-hand corner an American warship was sinking beneath the water. The message on the billboard read: LOOSE LIPS SINK SHIPS.

The billboard was a vivid reminder of the war to the

people who came to the ballpark to forget it for the du-ration of the game. Christine wondered if it also re-minded Willy about his son Joey, who was on a ship like that somewhere in the Pacific.

"Hey, Tina!" A loud voice called from the sidewalk. Christine looked down to see Arlene's face peering up. She was carrying a wooden box and some pieces of cardboard that looked like the sheets Mr. Chin put in dress shirts to keep them from wrinkling.

"Guess what?" Arlene shouted with excitement. "I've already sold six tickets! My brother Jim and two of his friends want tickets to the first Brooklyn Dodgers game. And I saw Mr. Zeman in the street," she said, pausing to catch her breath. Mr. Zeman was a widower who lived across the street from the Chins and knew almost as much about baseball as Willy. Still shouting louder than necessary, Arlene finished her report in a gasp. "Mr. Zeman bought a ticket to the Dodgers game and he wants a whole series ticket to the three Cardinals games when they come to town! We're already almost rich!"

Arlene arrived at the top of the stairs, puffing and red-faced from both the excitement and the climb. Christine met her in the doorway with a glass of Uncle Stanislaus's homemade root beer.

The two girls sat on the living room floor and made two signs advertising their box seats (as they had decided to call them) on the front of the cardboard rectangles Arlene had brought.

"I stole them out of Daddy's shirts that he wears to church," she confessed with a giggle.

While they listened to the game on the radio, they each made a sign that read:

SEE THE CUBS GAMES

AIR-COOLED AND SHADED BOX SEATS

ALL THE COMFORTS OF HOME AND THE GAME TOO

and below in smaller letters:

Front row: 20 cents   Back Row: 15 cents
Lemonade & Sandwiches Available at Reasonable
Rates
Bring Your Own Beer

From another piece of cardboard, they cut small rectangles and carefully printed on them "Front Row" or "Back Row," and below, the date of the game. They made eight tickets for each of the next five scheduled home games. When they were finished, Arlene counted out the six tickets she had already sold, and they put the remaining tickets in the old cigar box Arlene had brought from home. They stored the signs on the shelf of the front closet.

While the Cubs were away during the following week, the two girls walked up and down the streets around Wrigley Field with their signs and their cigar box of tickets, looking for familiar faces of men they knew who had not enlisted or been drafted into the armed forces. Before the Cubs had even returned to Chicago, they had sold out the forty tickets they had printed for the next home stand.

At the end of the week, they counted their money. Seven dollars – and for only five games.

"Gee, how come we didn't think of this before?" Arlene moaned. She counted out her half and tucked it inside her shirt. "We could be millionaires by now!"

Christine jingled the coins in the palm of one hand. She had never heard such a pleasing sound. The coins felt cool and smooth against her skin. After Arlene left, she stuffed the bills and coins into the toe of one of her penny loafers. She was almost one-quarter of the way to buying the winter coat for Mama. Just wait until Christmas when Mama opened the box from Sears, Roebuck. Christine could picture her carefully untying the ribbon and winding it into a neat roll as she always did.

"Hurry, Mama!" she would shout, trying not to give away her secret. "Open it! Don't worry about the ribbon!"

And then Mama would pull off the lid, fold back the tissue – and there would be the coat in all its splendor.

Christine could just imagine the look of astonishment and delight on Mama's face. Arlene was right. They should have thought of this long ago.

For the two Dodgers games, all went well. Rosie left the apartment at noon. At twelve-thirty Arlene arrived with a loaf of bread and a pound of bologna. They stood the mattress on end against the brownstone wall of the building, and Christine set the eight chairs in two neat rows as Arlene handed them through the window.

When the porch was arranged, they went into the kitchen. Christine squeezed lemons while Arlene made bologna sandwiches on white bread, some with mayonnaise, some with mustard. While Christine sparingly mixed sugar into the lemonade in a glass pitcher, Arlene wrapped the sandwiches in waxed paper and piled them on a plate.

"Taste the lemonade," Christine said, handing a sample in the bottom of a jelly glass to Arlene.

Arlene took a sip. Her whole face puckered.

"Whew!" she said with a little shudder. "That's kinda sour."

"Well, it's the best I can do. I don't dare put in too much sugar because then I'd have to use some ration stamps, and Mama would notice. If they don't like it, we'll give them a refund."

They agreed on the price of five cents for a small glass of lemonade and twenty cents for a sandwich. Christine carried the plate of sandwiches and pitcher of lemonade into the living room and placed them on a table by the window with two little signs displaying the prices.

At one o'clock Jim Popelka arrived with his two friends, and the three of them took their places in the back row on the porch.

"Hey, this is swell!" Jim said, aiming a pair of binoculars over the right-field wall. "It's as good as being in the bleachers – and cooler, too. For once, you girls really came up with a good idea."

"Of course we did," Arlene replied, giving him her haughtiest look. "We're not idiots, you know."

Each of the boys bought a sandwich, and Christine was heading for the kitchen to replenish the supply just as Mr. Zeman arrived at the door.

"Good afternoon," he said with a formal bow to Christine and handed her one of the tickets with the day's date printed on it. "I believe I have a front row box seat?"

"Oh, yes, Mr. Zeman," Christine said with a welcoming smile and pointed toward the window. "Go right on out to the porch. Arlene will show you to your seat. Refreshments will be served momentarily," she added, in what she hoped was her most adult manner. Mr. Zeman bowed again and headed toward the window as Christine started once more for the kitchen.

From then until the game ended at a quarter past four, the girls hardly had time to stop and draw a deep breath. A few of the men brought their own beer, but the rest drank lemonade. Nobody complained, but Christine noticed after everyone had left that none of the Dixie cups they used for the lemonade had been emptied.

"The sandwiches were a hit," Arlene said, surveying the empty plate. "We'll have to make more next time."

"I forgot about the bathroom getting so much use," Christine said as she ruefully surveyed the toilet with its raised seat. "Men sure are messy." She wiped the toilet and sink with a rag and threw the dirty towel the men had used into the hamper.

The girls put everything in order and counted out the day's take. Two dollars and fifty cents even. The bread, bologna, and lemons had cost a dollar, leaving them each with an additional seventy-five cents profit. With a little shiver of anticipation, Christine added it to the money in her shoe.

By the time the Saint Louis Cardinals arrived in town two days later, the girls' routine was down to a system. Fifteen minutes before game time they were awaiting their box seat holders when they heard a knock at the door.

"Come on in – " Christine started to say as she opened the door but stopped in midsentence. Mrs. Fazio stood in the doorway.

"I'm glad you're home, Christine," she said with a smile that added two extra chins to her plump face. "I was hoping maybe you could stay with the twins for an hour or so this afternoon. It's Tillie's day off from giving shampoos and sets and turning ugly ducklings into swans." She gave a little laugh that ran up and down the scale. "And we thought we'd take in a matinee."

She peered over Christine's shoulder to Arlene, who stood in the living room holding the plate of sandwiches. "Arlene would be welcome too, of course," she added, and the rolls of flesh jiggled in agreement. By now, everyone in the building knew Arlene.

"Gee, Mrs. Fazio, I'm sorry we can't this afternoon. We're kind of busy." Christine paused, but Mrs. Fazio was still staring at Arlene and the sandwiches. "Next week I could."

Mrs. Fazio pulled her eyes back to Christine and smiled again, but this time her lips barely moved.

"Yes, it looks like you're very busy. Well, perhaps next week then." She turned to go.

At the top of the stairs, she met Mr. Zeman and two of his friends climbing up from the flight below.

"Good afternoon," Mr. Zeman said politely and tipped his hat as he passed her on the stairs.

"Good afternoon," his friends echoed as they too passed by.

Mrs. Fazio stared after them with open mouth as the men turned down the hallway and entered the apartment. Then she hurried down the stairs.

The following day, when noon came and went and Rosie hadn't yet awakened, Christine grew anxious. It hadn't occurred to her to tell Rosie about the new business because Rosie was so seldom at home.

The two girls were still working in the kitchen when the men began to arrive twenty minutes before game time.

"Hi, Mr. Zeman," Christine said as she opened the door. "Go on out and take a seat. We'll have the sandwiches ready in just a few minutes."

"No hurry, Christine. Take your time." He held up a brown paper sack. "We brought beer today, so will have no need for your delicious lemonade." He marched through the living room followed by his two friends, and the three men disappeared through the window.

By the time the last ticket holder had arrived, the two teams were lined up in front of the dugouts, blue and red caps held uniformly over white and gray chests. "The Star-Spangled Banner" began to play.

Just as the last note ended with the roll of a drum, Rosie's door flew open.

"Christine!" she hissed loudly from inside the bedroom. "Come here!"

Christine knew from the vehemence of the hiss that Rosie was not in a good mood. Rosie's being at home was definitely a handicap they had not foreseen. With a sinking feeling, Christine approached the doorway. Rosie stood in the darkened room, her bathrobe wrapped tightly around her. The shade was pulled slightly askew as though lowered in a hurry.

"Christine, what in heaven's name is going on? Why are all those men here?"

"They've come to see the game. They all have tickets to sit on our porch."

"What a harebrained scheme! How could you sell our home?"

"I'm not selling our home, just seats on the porch!" Christine said. "You never go out there, anyway."

"Don't you know you can't have a stream of old men parading in and out of our apartment every day?"

"Why not? We've already made almost eleven dollars. Just think what we can make by the end of the summer!" How like Rosie to want to spoil a good idea just because she hadn't thought of it first.

"They can see right in my window!" Rosie hissed again.

"You have the shade closed. They can't see," Christine countered. "Anyway, they're more interested in the game."

"You'll have to give the money back right now. I'll bet this is all your fat little friend's doing. What would Mama say?"

The mention of Mama set butterflies loose in Christine's stomach. Maybe she should have mentioned the business to Mama, told her about their idea. But Mama might have thought of all kinds of reasons for them not to do it. She would have worried, and there really was nothing to worry about. She would have wondered about the money, too, and made Christine put it in the bank. And that would have meant no new coat for Mama for Christmas.

"Why would Mama care?" Christine asked, trying to decide whether to continue the argument with Rosie or admit defeat.

She turned toward the kitchen to confer with Arlene when suddenly the front door flew open and Mama appeared like a dark thunderhead. She was carrying her umbrella with the onyx handle and held it poised to strike. At the same moment, Arlene came through the swinging door carrying the plate of sandwiches. She stopped short at the sight of Mama with the raised umbrella.

"Roseann! Christine!" Mama called from the open door. "Is all right?"

"Nothing's wrong, Mama," Christine said in a small voice.

"Roseann! Christine! Tell me in heaven's name, what are you girls doing?" She shouted in Polish and whanged the umbrella head hard against the door. It was her most prized possession and a clear indication she meant business.

Arlene backed behind the kitchen door, leaving Christine to face Mama alone.

At that moment, Rosie appeared in the bedroom door still clutching her bathrobe tightly around her.

"Don't blame me, Mama," she said. "I told Tina it was a crazy idea."

"Christine!" Mama shouted a third time. "What are you doing? Why are all these men in our home? What would your father say?"

Hearing the shouting, the men began to climb back through the window to see what all the commotion was about. Without waiting for an answer, Mama assaulted them.

"All of you! Out of here!" Mama shouted, waving her umbrella at them. "*Matka Boska!* Mother of God! Go from my house! Leave my daughters alone!"

"But, Mama, they can't!" Christine cried. "They've paid their money. We'll have to give it back."

"*Matka Boska!*" The umbrella rose again, and for a moment Christine thought perhaps Mama would strike her next. But Mama had spotted a familiar face in the group scrambling back through the window. "Mr. Zeman! What is a decent man doing in my daughter's bedroom? What is happening here? Would you be so good as to tell me?"

"It's the game, Mrs. Kosinski, the baseball game! It's not what you think! Oh, believe me, ma'am, it's not what you think!"

By this time, the seven other men had retreated down the stairway. Mr. Zeman started to follow.

"Wait, Mr. Zeman," Christine called after him. "You have to get your money back."

"No, no," he called as he headed for the stairs. "Keep the money. By all means, keep the money!"

Mama took a deep breath and turned to Christine. "Now, Christine, I take time from work. So first I must know what you and your little friend Arlene were doing."

"We sold seats to watch the ball game, Mama. The men were sitting out on the porch. We wanted to make some money." Christine had never seen Mama so angry before, and she was the cause of it.

"Baseball seats? What are you talking? How can this be?"

"It's true, Mama. There's a perfect view of the ball-park from my porch. All except right field." It suddenly occurred to her that Mama had never climbed out onto the porch to see. "And the best part is that it's shaded from the sun."

"So that is it?" Mama gave a deep sigh. "Well, Christine, I hope now you are learning that inviting men into our home is not a good way for making money."

"Yes, Mama."

"Arlene," Mama called in a loud voice. "You come out now from the kitchen." Slowly Arlene emerged from behind the kitchen door.

Rosie, who had been watching the scene from the safety of her bedroom door, suddenly laughed. "I'll have to give you both credit. Who else but you two would ever have dreamed of selling seats to watch the ball game from their front porch?"

Still laughing, Rosie disappeared into her bedroom to get dressed.

"Now, you two girls, no harm is done so we will not say more about it," Mama said. "But I think is best maybe you not be together so much for little while. I think you both need to get little more sense. Hmmm?"

"Yes, Mama," Christine said. Arlene nodded, a look of misery on her face.

"We shall say for two weeks?"

"Yes, Mama."

"Then I say enough." Mama sighed and turned to the door. "I must go back now, explain to Aronsons why I left so much in a hurry! They must think my house on fire, I run out so fast! Arlene, is time you go, too."

Arlene was out the door and down the stairs before Christine could say good-bye. Mama followed more slowly after her.

"Tomorrow, Christine," she said from the top of the stairs, "I think you must give back what monies you owe."

"Mama," Christine said from the doorway. When Mama paused to look up at her, Christine was relieved to see her face was no longer frowning and full of tight lines. "How did you find out?"

"Oh, a little bird called me at the Aronsons'. She say

whole parade of men go into our home. I thought it best I come myself, see what is happening here."

"Was it Mrs. Fazio, Mama?"

"Never you mind who. It's no matter now. All is over and done. Maybe you fix the supper for tonight. That will keep you out of trouble for a while." Shaking her head, but with the hint of a smile, Mama disappeared down the stairwell muttering, "Baseball, bah!"

Christine lifted the chairs back through the window and replaced them around the dining room table. Not only was their business gone, but tomorrow she would be bankrupt as well. And all because of Mrs. Fazio. Rosie was right. She deserved to be married to a man like Mr. Fazio.

With a sigh of regret, Christine went into the kitchen. She and Mama and Rosie would eat bologna sandwiches for supper that night.

In the middle of the night, Christine awakened from a nightmare. Papa was on the ship in the billboard across the street, trying to get to them from Poland. In the dream she had seen him slipping down the deck to the stern, which was already submerged in water.

She awoke shivering and wet to find the rain driving across the city from the west onto her porch. Trembling from the dream and the chill of the cold rain, she rummaged in the dark for the rubber poncho, pulled it across the mattress, and climbed through the window. Silently she made her way through the darkness down the hall to Mama's room. Still trembling, she slipped into the big bed beside Mama and snuggled under the covers.

Mama turned, half lifting her head out of drowsy sleep.

"Is that you, Christine?"

"Yes, Mama. It's raining and I had a bad dream. I dreamed. . ." Christine's voice trailed off. Telling Mama the dream would only worry her. She felt Mama's arm go around her and she snuggled into the warm curve.

"Is all right now?"

"Yes, Mama." Christine listened as Mama's breathing began to deepen. "Mama?"

"Hmmm?"

"I'm sorry about the baseball tickets, about today. I didn't mean to worry you, Mama."

"I know. Is over and forgotten. Sleep now, *mala* Christine. Morning comes soon."

"Good night, Mama," Christine whispered, and she closed her eyes to shut out the darkness.

9

◆ ◆ ◆ ◆ ◆

Soda Jerk

Christine stacked the dog-eared copies of *Photoplay* and *Silver Screen* into a neat pile and placed them on the table she had just dusted between the two hair dryers in Tillie's front room. Sighing, she glanced at the enameled clock on the shelf above Tillie's work station and looked around for something else to do. She had already dusted the glass shelves that held the shampoo and wave set lotion and wiped out the shampoo bowl.

This Saturday time had stood still. Mama was at the Aronsons', Rosie was upstairs catching up on her sleep while the Cubs were on the road, Arlene was off limits for another week, and even Mrs. Himmelstein was out for the day visiting her niece from Evanston. With the Cubs out of town, Willie's corner was deserted, and the streets surrounding the ballpark seemed strangely silent. It would be three more weeks before school started, but Christine was almost looking forward to an end of summer.

By the middle of the morning, she had grown tired of being alone in the apartment and made her way down the narrow cement stairs beneath the stoop to Tillie's beauty salon in the basement. Most of Tillie's customers were older women from the neighborhood who had time for standing appointments and looked forward to sharing the neighborhood gossip. Tillie preferred the basement apartment so her customers would have fewer steps to climb.

Mrs. Bertacchi sat under one of the dryers while Tillie, curling a strand of hair around her finger and fastening it in place with a bobby pin, set the hair of a woman Christine didn't know. With the woman's wet hair pinned tightly to her head, she looked to Christine like a scrawny plucked chicken.

Tillie, as broad as the chair was wide, had thick, bright red hair that swept up like a bird in flight into a cluster of curls on top of her head. Mama disapproved of the fact that Tillie was a divorcée, but every Christmas Tillie gave them a gift box with a bottle of shampoo for Christine, lipstick or nail polish for Rosie, and a bar of Yardley's lavender soap for Mama.

Sometimes, in the early hours of summer mornings, Christine was awakened by voices as Tillie returned from an evening on the town with a date.

"Aw, come on, Tillie, just for a little while." The

rumble of a man's voice would drift up to the porch in the early morning stillness, followed by the familiar sound of Tillie's muffled laughter.

Sometimes after the door had closed with a creak and a clang of the metal latch, the sound of a man's footsteps would echo down the block and around the corner. But sometimes Tillie's door opened and closed followed by silence on the street. Christine never mentioned those times to Mama.

Now Tillie settled the woman under the second dryer and paused at her desk to check her appointment book.

"Oh, pshaw," she said, picking up a brown bottle and peering at the bottom. "Mrs. Martin's coming in later for a touch-up, and I'm outta bleach. Christine, honey, be a love and run up to Peavy's for a bottle of peroxide, would you?"

"Sure, Tillie." Christine's eyes lit up. The day suddenly looked brighter.

"And bring back a quart of chocolate ice cream," Tillie added, handing Christine a dollar from the cash drawer. "It's gonna be another hot night. We'll have some out on the stoop after supper."

At the drugstore, Christine noticed that the sultry woman in red still lounged in the window on the white bearskin rug, but by now the sun had faded the crimson nails and dress to a pale salmon. The woman's creamy skin was blotched with stains where moisture had con-

densed behind the glass and dripped onto the cardboard. The bearskin rug was dotted with flyspecks. It
was time Mr. Peavy asked Chen Yu to send him another
woman.

As she stepped through the door, Christine glanced
toward the soda fountain. At first she thought no one
was there, but then Peter Horner suddenly appeared
from behind the lemonade dispenser. With a quick
surge of lightness, Christine floated across the polished
surface of the floor to the back of the store where Mr.
Peavy was at work stocking the shelves with bottles of
Bromo Seltzer and milk of magnesia.

"I need a bottle of peroxide, please, Mr. Peavy," she
said, fishing the dollar bill from her pocket.

"Going to be the next Betty Grable, are you, Christine? Does your mom know about this sudden transfor-
mation?"

Mr. Peavy made Christine nervous. She never knew
if he was joking or not. "It's not for me, Mr. Peavy," she
said, shifting her weight from one foot to the other. "It's
for Tillie. Mrs. Martin's coming for a touch-up."

"Well, that's okay then. We certainly wouldn't want
to disappoint Mrs. Martin's roots, would we?"

"No, sir," Christine answered with a little smile, sure
this time Mr. Peavy was making a joke.

He reached for a bottle of peroxide, slipped it into a
paper sack, and handed it to Christine with sixty-five
cents change.

"Tell Tillie she shouldn't send a girl to do a woman's work. Tell her next time she should come herself."

Christine thought she saw Mr. Peavy wink, but before she could be certain, he had turned back to the cartons he was unpacking.

With hesitant steps, Christine approached the soda fountain. She stood on one foot and leaned against the marble top, watching while Peter made root beer floats for a man and woman at one of the small tables. The root beer foamed over the top of the glasses and ran down the sides in sudsy rivulets, just like the ice cream soda Oompah had bought her years ago.

After setting the floats on the table, Peter returned to the counter.

"Rosie's sister," he said with a smile of recognition. "Christine, isn't it?"

Christine nodded dumbly, saved from the necessity of a reply by the entrance of a little girl pulling an older woman through the door behind her. The girl climbed onto a stool midway down the counter and started spinning in circles.

"Priscilla, you'll make yourself sick doing that," the woman said in a tired voice, stretching out one arm to halt the next revolution. "If you want ice cream, you'll quit that right now."

Peter glanced at them without moving. "What can I get you, Christine?"

"Take care of them first," she said, gesturing to the

pair at the counter. "I'm in no hurry." She was happy for a reason to stay and watch.

Peter wrote their order on a little yellow pad and then took an oval silver dish from beneath the counter. He peeled a banana, cut it in half lengthwise, and placed the two pieces side by side in the dish. Lifting an ice cream dipper from a container of water, he scooped three neat balls of ice cream from bins beneath the counter – a scoop of chocolate, one of vanilla, and one of strawberry.

In quick succession, he dipped syrup from three recessed containers beneath the wide mirror across the back wall – first chocolate syrup on the vanilla ice cream, then strawberry on the chocolate ice cream, and pineapple on the strawberry ice cream. He finished it off with three dollops of whipped cream, a sprinkling of nuts across the top, and right in the center a single glistening red cherry. The banana split was a work of art. Christine's mouth watered.

Peter set the dish between the woman and child and placed a spoon at either side.

"Thanks for waiting," he said as he turned back to Christine. "What can I do for you now?"

"A quart of chocolate, please. Hand-packed." Christine watched as he took an empty cardboard container and began to scoop chocolate ice cream from the bin. He never wasted a motion or took an unnecessary step.

She couldn't imagine any better job than being a soda jerk.

"That looks like fun," she said with a wistful sigh.

"Yeah, it's okay. After a while, though, I guess it's like any job. You do it pretty much without thinking. What keeps it interesting is trying to make each order just a little bit better than the last one. Mr. Peavy doesn't settle for second best."

"I think a soda would be the most fun."

"That's probably the hardest to do just right because you don't measure the syrup or the soda water. You have to do it all by eye. The most important thing, though, is you have to mix a spoonful of vanilla ice cream into the syrup before you add the soda water. Then you fill it up halfway, mix it real good, and add two scoops of ice cream. To finish it off, you put in another little squirt of syrup and fill it the rest of the way with more soda water. Now that's the way to make a great soda," he ended with pride in his voice.

Peter folded the sides of the cardboard lid over the top of the heaped mound of ice cream and pushed down with the palm of his hand on the rounded dome.

"Say," he said suddenly as he handed her the carton in a brown paper bag. "Would you maybe want to work here just for tonight?"

"Me?" Christine's heart turned over.

"Sure. I really could use some help. Cathy O'Hoolihan just called in sick, and Saturday night's our busiest time. It would just be for tonight."

"I don't know how. I've never done it before."

"That's no problem. It's not hard. I could teach you everything in half an hour. Mr. Peavy can't hire anybody under fifteen, but if you were here just kinda helping out for one night, it wouldn't be a problem. Would you like to do it?"

"Would I? Sure I would!" It was beyond her wildest dreams, better even than catching Phil Cavaretta's home run.

"That's great," Peter said. His smile reminded Christine of how nice it would be to spend an evening with him behind the counter. "That's a relief. I'd have a real hard time by myself. Come back around six, okay? I'll show you the ropes before it gets busy."

Christine nodded and headed for the door. "See you at six."

Outside, she paused to think about the evening ahead. A whole night of making sundaes, ice cream sodas, and malted milks. She would work hard, do a good job, and maybe when she was fifteen Mr. Peavy would hire her full-time.

She turned to the window. "See you later," she said, saluting the woman in red with the carton of ice cream. She hurried down the sidewalk toward home, unmindful of the humid afternoon, anxious to get to Tillie's and bursting with the need to share the news with someone.

A whole night working with Peter Horner. Wait until Arlene heard about it. She would be green with envy.

Mama wouldn't be home from the Aronsons' until after six. She would have to leave a note explaining where she was. Mama wouldn't mind. Being at Peavy's was as safe as being at home.

Christine crossed Waveland at a run. Breathless and perspiring, she jumped down the three little stairs under the stoop and flung open the door. The glass rattled in the pane.

Tillie jumped in surprise, her rolls of flesh jiggling in protest at the sudden move. Four eyes in two startled faces under the dryers widened and blinked in unison.

"Hey, Tillie!" Christine shouted. "You'll never guess what I'm going to do tonight!"

10

♦ ♦ ♦ ♦ ♦

Saturday Night
Soda Fountain

At exactly six o'clock, Christine drew a deep breath and walked through the door of Peavy's Rexall Drugstore. The bell jangled behind her. As she walked toward the counter where Peter stood talking to Mr. Peavy, her heart sank. Mr. Peavy wasn't going to let her work there after all. He was going to send her home again.

"Right on the dot," he said looking up at her with a nod, acknowledging her arrival. "Peter tells me you're filling in for Cathy tonight."

"Yes, sir," Christine said, nodding her head to help urge him into agreement.

"Well, that's fine. Peter's happy to have the help. But you understand, it's on the q.t., strictly unofficial. I don't want the Labor Relations boys on my neck." Christine nodded again. "You think you can handle it all right? Saturday nights get busy in here."

"Oh, yes, sir!" Her head bobbed like a cork on water.

"Well, Peter knows the ropes. Just do what he tells you and you shouldn't have a problem." Mr. Peavy turned on his heel, doing a quick about-face like a soldier on parade, and disappeared into the rear of the store.

Peter handed Christine a large white apron. "Better start with this," he said. "You'll need it. Not afraid to get a little messy, are you?"

Christine shook her head. Peter motioned her behind the counter. Slowly she walked around the end and entered the unexplored territory behind it. Too late now to turn back.

Step by step, leading her slowly from one end of the counter to the other, Peter showed her where everything was located, from the cash register at one end to the array of freshly washed glasses and dishes stacked in a careful pyramid at the other. In between lay the bins of ice cream, spigots for soft drinks and soda water, containers of syrups, jars of maraschino cherries and chopped nuts, two malted-milk blenders, inverted stacks of cones, and a bunch of ripe bananas.

At the end of the counter, Peter pointed to the dishes and glasses. "Round dishes for sundaes," he said, "oval for banana splits. Do you know how to make a banana split?"

Christine nodded. "I watched you make one earlier today."

"Sundaes are easy. Just ice cream and toppings, one scoop or two. They'll tell you what flavor. No extra charge for whipped cream and nuts. Don't forget the cherry." He pointed to a sign behind the counter that held little removable letters and numbers. "Everything we have is listed there," he explained, "and all the prices. When you wait on a group of people at one of the tables, take a pad and write down the order. Otherwise it's easy to forget. For people at the counter, you can take them one at a time so it's no problem."

Christine nodded.

Peter moved down another few feet and pointed to the rows of glasses. "Regular glasses for Cokes and lemonade, large or small. The tall, fat glasses in the silver holders are for floats and ice cream sodas. For floats it's almost always root beer. Two scoops of vanilla in the glass and fill it up with root beer."

In the front of the store the bell jangled, and a woman wandered over and sat at the counter, the first customer of the evening.

"Go ahead," Peter whispered to Christine. "I'll watch you. Don't be nervous."

But she *was* nervous and prayed she didn't look as scared as she felt. Christine approached the woman, but before she could ask for the order, the woman said, "Butterscotch sundae with coffee ice cream."

Christine breathed a sigh of relief. The woman had believed she really was a soda jerk.

"One scoop or two?" Christine remembered to ask.

"Two."

"Whipped cream and nuts?"

"Sure. Might as well get hung for a sheep as a lamb." The woman laughed heartily at her own joke. Christine smiled in return. This wasn't so hard.

"Water," Peter prompted quietly from where he stood a few feet away. Christine filled a small glass with ice water and set it in front of the woman, who had taken a copy of *Ladies' Home Journal* from her shopping bag and was already engrossed.

Christine lifted down a sundae dish, located the bin with the coffee ice cream, and picked up the scoop from the container of water. Carefully she dipped it into the ice cream and then twice again, adding more ice cream with each dip until the scoop held a well-rounded ball. She placed the ice cream in the dish, added a second scoop, and then moved to the heated container marked *Butterscotch*, dipping one ladleful on top of the ice cream. She paused and glanced up at Peter with a questioning look.

Peter nodded his head, holding up two fingers. Christine dipped the ladle into the hot butterscotch a second time. She squirted on a crown of whipped cream in a neat circle and added a sprinkling of nuts and finally the all-important cherry. She looked at Peter. He nodded again, making a circle of his thumb and first finger to show his approval.

Christine set the dish carefully in front of the woman and placed a spoon beside it. She looked at it with pride. It was a beautiful sundae, neat and symmetrical, and she had made it. She smiled with pleasure. This wasn't work. This was fun, more fun even than roller-skating.

"That was perfect," Peter said. "I couldn't have done it any better myself. You're a natural. I'll show you how to make an ice cream soda, and then you're on your own." Christine glowed at the pride in his voice.

By the time he had demonstrated the steps of making a soda, the next customers had settled onto the stools at the counter. "Go get 'em, tiger," Peter whispered. "Remember, just yell if you need help." He gave her a quick pat on the back and turned his attention to one of the customers.

From that point on, Christine was caught up in the flurry of a summer Saturday night at the soda fountain. Every now and then, as they worked together, she was aware of Peter standing beside her or passing back and forth behind her, but she was far too busy to pay much attention.

By eight o'clock the perspiration began to trickle down her neck. She paused only long enough to wipe it with a wet towel. People came and went in a steady stream. There was no longer time to feel nervous about what she was doing. As soon as she had completed one order, Christine turned to the next. A tin roof sundae with Hershey's chocolate syrup and Spanish peanuts. Hot fudge sundaes with lots of whipped cream and extra nuts. Lemonades and root beer floats. Double ice cream cones with chocolate sprinkles on top.

At last, shortly before nine o'clock, she took her first order for ice cream sodas, one chocolate, one strawberry. Hers would be perfect sodas. Carefully she slipped two glasses into silver holders and pumped syrup into the bottom, three good squirts for each glass. She moved through the litany she had memorized – was it only three hours ago?

She placed the two sodas on the counter in front of an army corporal and a girl about Rosie's age. The flavored foam seeped over the rim of the glasses and down the sides just as it had with her own first soda. With a feeling of satisfaction, she watched as the soldier with the chocolate soda bent over his straws, sucked deeply, and swallowed.

He looked up with a smile. "Hey, this is great. Best soda I've had." Christine smiled back. Being a soda jerk was even better than she had imagined.

The rest of the evening passed in a blur of faces and orders, a steady stream of syrup and soda water. At first, when making change, Christine had to pause and think about what she had learned in arithmetic class, how to start at the amount of the purchase and then count upward from pennies to dollars until she reached the amount the customer had given. But as the evening progressed, she found she could do it without thinking about it.

As the soda fountain grew busier, the drugstore became warmer, filled with people waiting for a table or a stool at the counter, browsing through the aisles of merchandise. Christine could no longer feel the breeze moving back and forth between the two fans. She had long ago lost track of her wet towel and didn't take time to find another, using instead a corner of her apron, her shirt sleeve, or sometimes just the back of her hand to wipe the perspiration from her forehead.

She moved in a continuous round between the tables, the counter, and the island of equipment against the back wall. Gradually, though, first one then another of the tables emptied, and no one slipped in to fill the vacant chairs. The counter suddenly was only half-filled, and everyone had been served.

Behind the counter Christine paused and poured herself a glass of ice water, grateful for the moment of rest. She held the glass against her forehead until a little shiver ran down the base of her spine, then lowered it to her lips and drank it down in one long gulp. The clock above the counter read a quarter past ten. Only fifteen minutes to closing time. The night was ending. She wished it were only beginning.

Christine leaned back against the ice cream bins. Her legs ached from her toes to her thighs. Even her hip bones hurt. She wiggled her arms and shoulders to loosen the tight muscles. But it was a nice tiredness, the feeling that comes after working hard at a pleasant task. If she were asked, she would gladly start all over again.

Peter rinsed his hands under the faucet and leaned beside her as he dried them with a towel.

"Busy night, huh?" He glanced at her from the corner of his eye. "I can finish up now. Why don't you go on home?"

She shook her head, almost too tired to answer but determined not to quit a minute before he did. "I'll help clean up."

"You did okay, kid. One of you is worth two Cathy O'Hoolihans any day of the week." He put his arm around her shoulders and gave her a little squeeze. "And don't forget it, you hear?"

Peter's words were a magic wand waved above her head. The soreness dissolved, the aching muscles eased. One word of praise from him was more than enough payment. This was the best night of her life. Papa would have been proud of his daughter tonight. He probably still thought of her as a little girl and would be surprised to see how grown-up she was.

"Just ten more minutes and we can both go home," Peter said as he began to clear the remaining glasses off the counter.

With a sigh, Christine turned to the sink full of dirty

dishes just as the jangling of the bell signaled another customer.

"Wouldn't you know," Peter muttered. "Right before closing time." He looked up from the sink toward the door and his face suddenly brightened. "Hey, Christine, it's your sister!"

11

♦ ♦ ♦ ♦ ♦

Banana Split

In surprise, Christine looked up to see Rosie heading for one of the tables with a marine lieutenant in dress uniform. Mama and Tillie followed close behind, and the marine pulled out a chair and held it for Mama as she sat. Peter went to the table with an order pad. Rosie smiled at him and said a few words but pointed across the counter at Christine.

"They want only that world-famous soda jerk, Christine Kosinski, to wait on them," he said with a sheepish grin as he returned to the counter. "Some people have all the luck."

With reluctance Christine took the order pad and started toward the table. It was one thing to serve a table full of strangers, quite another to wait on her own family, especially in the company of a good-looking marine. For the first time since she had begun four hours earlier, Chrisine felt a nervous flutter in her stomach.

"Hello, Mama. Tillie. Hi, Rosie," Christine said with a nervous laugh as she approached the table. Mama's eyes grew very round. She bent her chin into her chest and made a sound that sounded very much like a smothered laugh. Christine shifted from one foot to the other and then back again.

"Well, if it isn't the world-famous Madame Kosinski, queen of the soda fountains," Rosie said with a laugh. "Chris, meet Chris. Christine, this is First Lieutenant Christopher O'Malley of the United States Marine Corps."

With his white cap tucked under one arm, the lieutenant stood and gave a little bow in her direction. In his neat blue trousers with the red stripe and darker blue jacket with gold trim, he looked very distinguished.

"Hi," Christine said. She felt awkward in front of this big man with hair almost as red as Tillie's.

Suddenly Mama looked up, laughing and shaking her head.

"Tillie, what is this vision we see? Is possible this is my daughter who is head to toe in chocolate?"

"It's nobody I ever saw before," Tillie said, joining in the laughter.

Christine looked down at herself. Mama was right. Chocolate was everywhere. All over her skirt, her apron, her shirt sleeves. Even her left sock had a brown smear across the top. She turned to look in the mirror above the back counter. Even at a distance she could see dark streaks and smudges crisscrossing her face. Strands of brown hair that had pulled loose from her braid fell across her forehead and stuck to her damp temples. She was a mess.

"Is all right," Mama said in a more sober voice. "Is clear you are working very hard this evening. At home we will put you in the bathtub, clothes and all."

Christine wanted to tell them how busy she and Peter had been, how there hadn't even been time to wash her sticky hands, much less be careful about her clothes, but somehow the words wouldn't come. She was too tired now to care about a little chocolate even for a United States Marine.

"We're just here to walk home with you, hon," Tillie said, no longer laughing. "When your mom read your message, she wanted to come so I tagged along."

"I'll be finished in a few minutes. Would you like something?"

"Tillie and I just finished chocolate ice cream at home," Mama said, shaking her head.

Rosie raised her curved eyebrows with a querying look in the direction of the marine.

"What's your specialty here?" he asked Christine with a smile.

Christine thought for a moment. "Banana splits," she replied suddenly. It was the only thing she hadn't made all night.

"Then banana split it is. With two spoons." He winked at Rosie, who laughed, puffing out her cheeks and patting her flat stomach.

Christine returned to the counter, where Mr. Peavy was counting the night's receipts.

"They want a banana split," Christine said to Peter as she lifted down one of the long oval dishes.

"You look kinda bushed. Do you want me to make it?"

"Oh, no. I'll do it. It's my first one." This would be her best, her finest achievement, and something to impress Mr. Peavy, too.

She thought about the way Peter had made the banana split that afternoon and locked each step firmly in her mind. First she tore the best banana from the bunch and carefully peeled it. She sliced it down the middle and laid the two halves side by side in the dish. Next she scooped three large round balls of ice cream—vanilla, strawberry, and chocolate—being careful to rinse the scoop after each flavor.

On each scoop she poured a generous dipperful of topping, then covered the top with swirls of cream in the form of petals, crowning each of the three scoops with a thick blossom of heavy white cream. She finished off the concoction with a sprinkle of chopped nuts and three cherries, one in the center of each whipped-cream flower.

"Look," she said with pride, holding the banana split

up for Peter to admire. She had never seen anything so magnificent, almost too beautiful to eat, truly a work of art and a fitting end to a perfect night.

"Look, Mr. Peavy!" she said and swung around to show him her masterpiece. The end of the dish glanced off the side of Mr. Peavy's arm. In one graceful motion, the bananas and ice cream sailed off the end of the dish and landed intact on the floor, hardly even disturbed by their flight and sudden landing. The three red cherries were still firmly anchored in the centers of the three whipped-cream flowers.

Christine could only stand and stare at the disaster on the floor. How could this have happened, especially now, with her family here and Rosie's marine and Mr. Peavy looking on? She stared at a crack in the floor beside the banana split. Pineapple syrup slowly oozed toward the crack. She wished she could disappear through the crack with it.

Peter was the first to react. He reached for a wide spatula and stooped down to begin scooping it off the floor.

"Don't worry, Christine," Peter said. "It's happened to all of us. I hate to tell you how many things I've spilled a whole lot worse than this. Isn't that right, Mr. Peavy?"

"Sure," Mr. Peavy replied. His voice seemed to come from a distance. "Don't worry. It wasn't your fault, Christine. Clumsy me, I got in your way."

"I'm sorry, Mr. Peavy. I'm so sorry." Suddenly so weary she wondered how much longer her legs would hold her, Christine knelt beside Peter and began to wipe the floor with a damp rag.

"I'll get this, Christine," Peter said gently, still on the floor. "You make another banana split, and I'll worry about the cleaning."

Christine felt tears spring to her eyes from the kindness in his voice. She wished he wouldn't be so kind.

"No harm done, Christine," Mr. Peavy said. "Just make another one and don't worry about it. Peter's right. Happens all the time. Goes with the territory. There's no use crying over spilled ice cream." Chuckling at his little joke, he headed toward the back of the store.

Numbly, Christine pulled herself to her feet. All the customers had left now except for the group at the table. She glanced over at them, afraid of inviting their sympathy as well. But they were engrossed in conversation, apparently unaware of the disaster behind the soda fountain. That at least was some consolation.

By rote she went through the motions of making another banana split and carried it to the table on a tray with two spoons and four glasses of water. Always a glass of water, Peter had instructed early in the evening, a lifetime ago.

"Hey, this looks great," Christopher said as he lifted a spoon.

"You're full of surprises, Christine," Rosie said with a smile. "I didn't know you had such hidden talents."

"You look tired," Mama said. "It's past bedtime."

"In a minute, Mama. As soon as we finish cleaning up."

She walked back to the counter and worked silently beside Peter until the dishes were washed and dried and stacked. She was too tired to worry about making conversation with him.

"I'll get their dishes," Peter said, nodding in the direction of the table where the marine was finishing the last bite of banana. "You look bushed. Why don't you go on home with your mom?"

Christine took off her apron and laid it on the counter. Looking at it, she had to smile. Mama was right. She was all over chocolate.

"Thanks a lot for letting me help, Peter," she said and held out her hand. "I really enjoyed it."

Peter took her hand, shook it once and held it.

"I'd have been sunk without you. You were terrific. And that was a really great-looking banana split. Far too good for anybody to eat!" He smiled and gave her hand a squeeze. The memory of the banana split sailing out of its dish faded away.

In a happy daze, Christine turned toward the table where Mama and Tillie were collecting their purses. It had been the best night of her life, a night she would never forget. And maybe, sometime in the future, Mr. Peavy might let her fill in again just for the fun of it. She would be the best soda jerk in the world, but not as a paying job, not for money. Only for the joy of it, for the pleasure of concocting those wonderful dishes, of creating each one just a little better than the last.

"Time for us all to be in bed," Mama said, lifting a loose strand of Christine's hair and smoothing it behind her ear.

Christine tucked her hand into Mama's and let herself be led toward the door. Her calves and thighs trembled from fatigue. The five blocks to Sheffield and Waveland would seem like five miles tonight.

"Christine!" Mr. Peavy called from the back of the store and hurried over to where they waited by the door. He pulled his hand from his pocket and held out two one-dollar bills. "This is for you. A token of my appreciation."

"Oh, no, Mr. Peavy," Christine said taking a step backward. "I didn't expect to be paid. I didn't do it for money."

"Nonsense," Mr. Peavy said with a little laugh, thrusting the bills toward her. "We did a record business tonight. You earned it, every penny of it."

"But I don't want to be paid, Mr. Peavy," Christine protested, feeling her eyes sting with tears. She couldn't cry now, not in front of Peter and Mama and Mr. Peavy. "I did it for the fun of it. For fun." Her voice shook.

"No, no, I insist. I won't have you going home empty-handed."

Mr. Peavy leaned forward and thrust the dollar bills into Christine's pocket, where they crackled behind the thin cotton fabric of her shirt. Not knowing what else to do, she turned to the door, wanting only to be gone, to be home and tucked into her bed on the porch.

"What do you say to Mr. Peavy, Christine?" Mama prompted softly.

Christine turned her head in the direction of Mr. Peavy. "Thank you, Mr. Peavy," she said in a dull voice, knowing she should sound more sincere. "Thank you very much for giving me two dollars."

"Don't mention it. You were a good little soda jerk, a real help to Peter."

Christine pulled open the door. The bell jangled behind her as she escaped into the sultry night air.

"I don't understand you, Christine," Rosie said behind her. "You'll sell baseball seats in your own home just to make some money, and then you turn down Mr. Peavy's money that you really earned." She shook her head in disbelief.

"But I didn't do it for money!" Christine took a deep breath to steady her voice. She would not let them know how much it hurt. They would laugh at her, call her silly for feeling this way. It was no good trying to explain. Even Mama would never understand that she felt betrayed. She didn't even understand it herself. She only knew that somehow the offer of money diminished the job she had done with such pleasure and such pride.

"Chris and I are heading uptown to the Aragon," Rosie said as the five of them clustered on the sidewalk outside the door.

"Nice to have met you all," Christopher O'Malley said, tipping his hat again. Together he and Rosie turned, disappearing into the crowd that still milled along the sidewalk on the summer Saturday night.

Christine turned with Mama and Tillie and started south on Sheridan Road toward home. Tonight she had worked as hard as any grown-up. Now she could understand why Mama looked so tired when she came home after a long day's work at the Aronsons' and sat for a while with her feet propped up. Now she knew how Mama felt. But if Papa had seen her at Peavy's tonight, he would have been amazed at what a good soda jerk his little girl was.

She was grateful, though, that the night was over at last. For once she had no interest in the Aragon Ballroom. For once on a Saturday night, she didn't even envy Rosie.

12

◆ ◆ ◆ ◆ ◆

A Night to Remember

When the sirens began to blow, Christine was sitting with Willy outside Wrigley Field. At first they heard the wail of a single siren from the station across the street on Waveland, but that siren was quickly joined by two others.

"Must be quite a fire," Willy remarked, looking up as though searching for flames in the sky.

Christine thought of the two bombs that had been dropped on those Japanese cities with the strange names of Hiroshima and Nagasaki just the week before. She wondered if Japan was seeking revenge with their own bombs, but before she could voice her fear to Willy, the sirens were joined by pealing church bells. They rang first from Saint Mary's a block to the east but were soon joined by the deeper bells from the Church of the Ascension to the west.

Christine lifted her head to listen. One by one, church bells from every direction joined in until the sound seemed to ring from every corner of the city. Christine looked at Willy in wonder. Inside the park a voice made an announcement on the loudspeaker, and a moment later a roar rose from within the encircling walls.

"By golly!" Willy cried out, shaking Christine's shoulder, "it must be the war. Tina, I think the war is finally over!"

He lifted her and swung her in a circle until her legs flew out behind her. "Whooeee, Tina!" he cried, setting her down with a great laugh. "It's gotta be over at last!"

Christine looked around her in a daze, not daring to believe what Willy was saying for fear it wasn't the truth. But deep in her heart she knew the moment they had so long awaited had finally arrived. The war was over.

Willy stood with his arm around her. "Thank God," he said. His voice was so quiet Christine barely heard him, but she could see his lips form the words. "Thank God."

Up and down the block, one by one doors opened and people swarmed onto the sidewalks from the houses, shops, and cafés that lined the streets. Radios blared from open doorways while excited broadcasters announced the news, but gradually their voices were lost in the shouts and laughter that joined the sirens and bells still ringing over the housetops.

Christine stood spellbound, not knowing whether to laugh or cry, wanting to do both at the same time. Surely now they would get word of Papa. Surely now someone who knew where he was or what had happened to him would somehow let them know. But for the first time since she and Arlene had skated through Graceland Cemetery, she let herself wonder if he might not be alive. The not knowing was hardest to bear.

"Now you'll hear somethin' about your dad, Tina," Willy said, as though reading her thoughts.

Christine turned to him with a smile and gave him a hug. "And now Joey can come home, Willy. That's just about the best news of all."

Across the street, Mrs. Bertacchi was standing on her stoop swinging a large brass dinner bell in a circle over her head. Next door Mr. and Mrs. Chin came out of their shop. Mrs. Chin held a baby in her arms wrapped in a blue blanket. She's had her baby, Christine thought in surprise, and I never even knew it. She felt a sudden pang of guilt that she had not stopped by to see them lately. She would take them the rattle and bib she and Mama and Rosie had bought for the baby. What better day to bring a gift to a new baby than the day the war ended?

By now the walkway around the park was crowded

with people hugging and kissing. Christine felt a hand grasp her elbow and turned to see Rosie's smiling face.

Rosie grabbed her around the waist, swinging her around and around in a circle, knocking into people with abandon, but nobody seemed to mind.

"Isn't it wonderful?" Rosie cried over the din of the crowd. "Isn't it just the greatest thing that ever happened? It's finally over! Now we'll know!" Rosie didn't mention Papa by name, but Christine knew who she was thinking of.

"Come on, Christine!" Rosie shouted. "Mama's probably on her way home. Everybody's been given the rest of the day off. The whole country is celebrating!"

Christine waved good-bye to Willy and followed Rosie through the crowd. Ahead, on their stoop, she saw everyone from the building standing together, shouting and waving. Tillie's red hair flashed in the sun. Even Mrs. Himmelstein was there waving an American flag on a stick.

"Great day! Great day!" Mrs. Himmelstein called as they neared the stoop. "Such news! Such news!" Christine ran up the steps and gave her a hug. "Ooof, Christine," she said with a laugh. "Be careful or you'll squeeze my gizzard out!"

Over Mrs. Himmelstein's shoulder she saw Mr. Fazio try to kiss Rosie on the mouth, but at the last second Rosie turned her head and the kiss landed on her ear instead.

Christine threw back her head and laughed again. Some things never changed.

"Come on, Christine," Rosie called to her later that evening after the supper dishes had been washed and put away. "This is no night to sit at home! Put on your dancing shoes. We're going to the Aragon Ballroom!"

"But will Mama let me?"

"On a night like this, who could say no? I promised to watch you like a hawk and bring you home early. She said, well, maybe just this once. . . ."

Before the words were out of Rosie's mouth, Christine was changing out of her dungarees and into a skirt. She had no dancing shoes, but she put on her still-shiny penny loafers. Not elegant, but they would do in a pinch.

She and Rosie rode the El uptown to Lawrence Avenue and walked across the crowded street to the entrance of the ballroom. Everyone in Chicago seemed to have come to the Aragon to celebrate the end of the war.

Rosie took Christine by the hand and led her right past the doorman into the teeming ballroom. He didn't seem to care.

The orchestra was playing "When the Lights Go On Again All Over the World." The room was filled with people already dancing, women in high-heeled shoes and young men in every uniform imaginable.

The fragrance of mingled perfumes had transformed

the room into a summer garden. Slowly, Christine looked around her. The Aragon Ballroom was exactly as Rosie had described it.

Rosie led her over to the railing entwined with crepe-paper flowers that separated the tables from the dance floor.

"Wait right here," Rosie said, and planted Christine beside a garlanded post. "I see Chris. I'll be right back. You'll be okay, won't you?"

Christine nodded and clung to her post, while Rosie dove into the sea of dancing bodies. A few minutes later, she resurfaced in the arms of the marine who had come with her to Peavy's, and they floated away together under the lights.

Christine looked up. Above the dance floor, the midnight blue sky imprinted with clusters of silver stars curved overhead. Right in the center hung the silver sphere, slowly spinning in time to the music, reflecting a ribbon of light that floated across the varnished floor and twined around the dancing couples.

At the far end of the room, the orchestra played behind a little railing. The men were dressed in identical azure blue suits with black lapels. A sign with silver letters announced that the music for dancing was "Styled by Chuck Stewart and His Starlight Orchestra."

Standing by her post, Christine yearned to be out there dancing. She would be the most graceful dancer

Chuck Stewart had ever seen. He would spot her in the crowd, ask her to dance a solo with her faceless partner. Space would clear just for them as the other dancers gathered around, watching her dip and turn in the bright shaft of the spotlight's beam. As the music ended, applause would rise in waves around her while she and her partner smiled and bowed.

"Wouldja like to dance?"

Startled, Christine's gaze dropped from the ceiling to the vague figure in front of her. "What?" she stammered.

"Wouldja like to dance? A few spins on the dance floor?"

Speechless, she stared at the speaker. He was a sailor, dressed in white middies, flared pants and white pullover shirt. A black tie was knotted at the base of the collar in the center of his chest.

The beat of the music slowed from a jitterbug to the familiar strains of "I'll Be Seeing You." Christine glanced at the sailor's eyes and quickly looked away. In desperation her eyes sought Rosie. She was out in the middle of the floor, twirling in a slow circle under the upraised arm of Lieutenant Christopher O'Malley. Rosie would be no help now. Christine looked back at the sailor, who watched her with a quizzical expression.

"Wouldja give me a dance?" he repeated. "Just for the fun of it?"

Christine stared at a spot below his chin. "Oh, no,"

she blurted out in a single exhalation. "No, I couldn't." She raised her eyes to a point just below the center of his face.

"Oh, come on," the sailor said with a smile. "How about a nice fox-trot?"

"I don't know how to do the fox-trot," Christine said. Her face flushed, and she looked away from him over the heads of the dancers on the floor. "I don't dance."

"Suit yourself," he said with a shrug and turned away.

Christine watched his retreating back. He was slender and straight, about Rosie's age, with curly dark hair cut short across the back of his neck. His smile had been nice. A little like Peter Horner's, she thought with a pang of regret.

The sailor stopped, turned abruptly, and took three steps back to where she stood.

"Anybody can do the fox-trot," he said smiling down at her. "It's easy. You wouldn't turn a war hero down, now would you?"

He reached out a hand and grasped hers that hung limply by her side. Without waiting for a reply, he pulled her toward the dance floor. "Don't worry," he said with a grin, "I'm not the big bad wolf. I won't gobble you up."

Too nervous to protest any further, aware of the feel of his hand holding hers, Christine allowed herself to be led onto the dance floor. Her heart was beating so loudly she hardly heard his voice when he spoke.

"We'll do the two-step," he said, looking down at his own feet. "I'll show you. It's not even really a step. You just move your feet back and forth in time to the music. Like this." In silence Christine watched as the sailor shifted his weight from one foot to the other and at the same time moved forward slowly. "See? There's nothing to it."

Pulling her toward him, he placed her left hand on his right shoulder and slipped his right arm around her waist. "Hang on. Here we go!"

In a single motion, he swung her out onto the dance floor. She stumbled once and righted herself, but he didn't seem to notice. Christine scrunched her eyes closed in her effort to concentrate on the music, listening only to it, to the slow beat of the song. Two steps. Back and forth. Back and forth. She stumbled again over the toe of his shoe as he maneuvered a turn. Her eyes flew open. He smiled down at her.

"You're doing fine," he said. "Relax. Enjoy it."

She took a deep breath and slowly exhaled, trying to relax and at the same time keep her mind on the direction he was moving. She felt the firm pressure of his hand in the center of her back and realized it was guiding her. His hand let her know where he would move next. If she paid attention, it was not so hard to follow.

She took another breath, counting the beat of the music inside her head, liking the feel of his fingers against her back.

His hand pressed tighter, and he turned her in place. This time she followed without stumbling. One by one her muscles began to relax. Dancing wasn't so hard. It was fun, almost like roller-skating, gliding across the dance floor, floating like a drift of cottonwood seed in the arms of a sailor.

"Say, what's your name?" The sailor's voice sounded husky in her ear.

"Christine." She dared to peek at his face and saw that his eyes were closed.

"Well, hi, Christine. I'm Ron."

"Are you really a war hero?" she asked shyly.

He threw back his head and laughed. "No, I'm afraid not! I just said that to get your sympathy. I enlisted in the navy a year ago and I've been at the Great Lakes Naval Station ever since. I haven't even been on a ship yet, and now it looks like I might not ever make it." He looked down at her upraised face with a smile. "Hey, you're not going to turn me down now, are you?"

"Oh, no," Christine said shaking her head.

"Good." His hand pressed more firmly against the small of her back, pulling her closer, lifting her onto her toes until his cheek brushed against her temple. His skin was smooth and smelled faintly of shaving lotion.

She felt the knot of his tie press against the side of her neck as he spun her in a full revolution, guiding her across the crowded floor through the press of swaying couples. And she was one of them. She was dancing with a sailor at the Aragon Ballroom, dancing cheek to cheek in a garden bower to the slow strains of the music on a warm summer night.

She closed her eyes, aware only of the touch of the sailor's cheek, the feel of his hand, the soft sound of his voice as he hummed the melody.

The orchestra swung into the last chorus, slowing the beat as it moved into the strains of the final lines of music.

The last note played, spiraling upward in the humid air. Christine opened her eyes and lifted her head. The ceiling curved, a dark blue sky filled with hundreds of twinkling stars. Rosie was right. It was like dancing under a shower of stars. And right in the middle the spinning silver sphere reflected a thousand little prisms of color.

The sailor's hand dropped from her back as he stepped back with a smile. "Say, that was swell, Christine."

He turned and led her through the milling couples to her post at the edge of the dance floor. "Thanks for the nice dance, Christine," he said, and with a wink and a wave of the hand he disappeared into the crowd.

Christine leaned against the column twined with paper roses. Her legs dissolved, her insides floated. If only the song had never ended.

She didn't even notice when Rosie came toward her through the crowd until she heard her voice calling to her.

"Hey, Christine! We saw you dancing. Aren't you the sly one? I leave you for a few minutes and the next thing I know you've hooked a sailor!" Rosie laughed and poked Christine in the ribs. "Not bad for your first trip to the Aragon!"

Christine blushed. The marine, Chris O'Malley, stood close to Rosie, his arm around her shoulder.

"We're going home now, Christine," Rosie said, her eyes glowing as light as her hair. "I've got some wonderful news. We're going to tell Mama, but I wanted you to be the first one to know." She smiled up at Chris, who was looking down at her. It was so clear they were in love, Christine wondered how she hadn't noticed. Seeing them together made her throat ache.

She wasn't even surprised when Rosie held out her left hand to display a small solitaire diamond ring on her fourth finger.

"Chris has asked me to marry him," Rosie said softly. "I'm going to be his wife." Tears glistened in her eyes and made them sparkle as though they, too, were set with diamonds. Above the dance floor the silver sphere continued its slow turn as the prisms of light and the diamond and Rosie's eyes all shimmered together.

Christine wrapped her arms around her sister and hugged her tight, catching the faint fragrance of Rosie's perfume, wanting never to let it go.

She had never seen Rosie filled with so much light.

13

♦ ♦ ♦ ♦ ♦

Plans and Preparations

By the first week in September, Christine was caught up in the plans and preparations for Rosie's wedding. Mama had forgiven Arlene for her part in the scheme of the box seats and said Christine could invite Arlene to the wedding and even to the reception afterward. Arlene's face had lit up with the anticipation of so much festivity.

At the first opportunity, Christine had also given Arlene a full account of her night at Peavy's Drugstore. Arlene's response had been exactly what Christine predicted – a little sympathy for the disaster of the banana split, and a lot of envy of Christine and regret that she herself had missed the chance to spend a whole night working beside Peter Horner.

"Oh, my gosh!" she had exclaimed, rolling her eyes and hitting her forehead with the heel of her hand.

"And to think that it might have been me! How un-lucky can a girl get!" But her disappointment had quickly faded with the news of Rosie's wedding and the assurance that she would not have to miss out on that occasion.

By the time school started, both girls were too excited by the upcoming event to dwell on what had happened during the summer. They rode the streetcar south and then walked two blocks west to Cermak Junior High School. The trip was uneventful, the cars noisy and crowded, grimy from the dirt that blew through the city.

After six years at Jane Addams Elementary School, Christine found the junior high immense, a maze of endless hallways on three floors. On the first day, she was sure she would get lost and might be left to wander the hallways, forever looking for the right classroom and always finding it just one period too late. But by the end of the week she wondered why it had ever seemed so large and forbidding. She discovered many old familiar faces from Jane Addams among her new classmates. And of course there was Arlene. By the end of the month, Christine felt as though she had been there forever.

Also by the end of September, the Cubs had officially won the National League pennant, an event that made starting junior high school seem pale by comparison.

The fact that the team was out of town when the pennant was clinched didn't stop the Wrigley Field fans from celebrating. A lot of beer flowed down the gutters on Clark Street that day.

The next time Christine saw Willy, his grin stretched ear to ear. Not only had the Cubs won the pennant, but he had also learned Joey would be discharged as soon as his ship docked sometime before the end of October.

Willy had taken Christine to see the newsreel of the signing of the peace treaty with Japan on board the battleship *Missouri* in Tokyo Bay. In the middle of the newsreel, he jumped up and shouted, "There he is! That's Joey!" He pointed in the darkness. "That's him. The third one from the left in the second row."

Christine squinted at the screen, but the faces of the sailors under their white caps all looked the same to her. She was happy for Willy, though, proud that her friend's son was on the ship where the proclamation of peace had been officially signed on September 2, V-J day, President Truman had called it, Victory over Japan.

During the first week of October, Christine sat on her porch with Arlene to watch the World Series. The weather had turned chilly, and they huddled in their coats and drank hot Ovaltine to keep warm. From their porch above right field, they cheered until their voices faded into raspy hoarse cries, but even so they couldn't help the Cubs win. The Cubs lost the World Series, but they had won the pennant, and somehow that seemed to be the most important victory.

On the final day, Willy packed up his remaining souvenirs to be stored over the winter in his small apartment until the following April, when he would dust them off and bring them out once more. He gave Christine a new set of photographs of all the team members who had played during the summer of 1945.

"This was a special team," he said. "They won the pennant. Maybe next year they'll win the Series, too." He gave her a hug. "See ya next year, Tina. Take care of yourself now, ya hear?"

"Sure, Willy. You too. Say hello to Joey when he gets home. See you next spring."

Neither of them mentioned Papa. Willy also had stopped saying "Soon, now."

Christine carried the set of photos upstairs and put them in her desk drawer. She threw out the stack Willy had given her the year before. She would hang the new ones later, after Rosie's wedding.

Rosie had quit her job at the factory, which in the future would be making nylon stockings instead of parachutes. Even Mama had taken two weeks off from work to spend more time at home helping Rosie. Sometimes Mama stopped in the middle of some task and just looked at Rosie. Christine knew she was thinking about what it would be like to have Rosie so far away. Chris O'Malley was being transferred to Quantico, Virginia, until his term of enlistment expired. Then he and Rosie would move to Cedar Rapids, Iowa, where his family owned a hardware business.

"It's not so far," Rosie had said, trying to soften the news when she first told them. "It's just a day's drive. We'll come visit you often."

"Of course you will," Mama said, but Christine saw her eyes fill with tears. A visit was not the same as living here. The apartment would seem empty with just the two of them.

But when she looked at Rosie, it was hard to feel very sad. Rosie's face glowed, and her laughter filled the apartment. The wedding would not be large, but all their relatives and neighborhood friends were invited, even the Fazios. Uncle Stanislaus would give Rosie away, and she would wear Aunt Sophie's wedding dress, which needed only a few minor alterations.

"It's amazing, isn't it," Aunt Sophie said with a laugh the day she brought the dress over to their apartment for Rosie to try. "Can you believe I ever could have fit into that?" With a sigh she patted her ample waistline. "But just look at the way it fits you almost like a glove!"

Rosie stepped out of her bedroom into the middle of the living room. The dress was white satin with a train that swept the floor and a white veil that drifted over the gown like mist.

Mama raised her fingers to her mouth as though at a

loss for words, but her eyes shone. Christine could only stand and stare at this fairy princess who was her sister.

"Oh, boy," she said at last. "Wait until Chris sees you in that dress. You'll knock him dead."

"Someday you can wear it, too, Christine," Aunt Sophie said with a smile.

Christine couldn't imagine herself in such a dress, much less getting married. For now she was happy to be maid of honor. Rosie had taken her shopping at Marshall Field's and bought her a new dress of blue velvet that looked like flowing water when it moved in the light. It was the nicest dress she had ever owned.

When it was time for Aunt Sophie to leave for the restaurant, Christine walked with her to the streetcar stop on Clark Street.

"Roseann will make a beautiful bride," Aunt Sophie said with a sigh. "I am only glad she has a real wedding dress to wear. All brides should have a wedding dress. It will be a perfect wedding. . . ." Her voice broke off. "Perfect, that is," she continued after a pause, "if her father were only here."

"Aunt Sophie, do you think Papa will ever come?" Christine asked. "Do you think he really is still alive?"

"Of course he is," Aunt Sophie replied and hugged Christine to her, burying Christine's face in the lapels of her wool coat. Christine caught the faint odor of cedar. "You musn't ever doubt that. For your mother's sake, and for Rosie's . . . and for yourself. We must all still believe he is alive. If we think it hard enough, it must be true."

"But the war with Japan has been over for a month, and the fighting in Germany ended in May. Wouldn't we have heard by now? Wouldn't he have found some way to let us know?"

"There could be many reasons. . . ." A little frown puckered the skin between Aunt Sophie's eyebrows and then smoothed away again. "You mustn't give up hope, little one. Until we know for certain what has happened, it is important to keep hoping. There is always time enough for grieving. Always time enough for that. . . ."

As she stepped up into the streetcar, Aunt Sophie turned to wave and smile. But Christine could see that she was worried, too. She had voiced her fears to Aunt Sophie so as not to worry Mama, but now she had worried Aunt Sophie instead. She must learn to keep her fears to herself, especially now that Rosie's wedding was near at hand. With a sigh, she turned to walk back to the apartment, where Mama and Rosie were still admiring the dress.

The week before the wedding, the weather turned warm again. Indian summer was Christine's favorite time of the year. It settled lazily over the midwestern plains as though biding its time, a wedding guest arrived too soon but in no hurry to move on.

Every morning the sun rose in a cloudless blue sky. A light breeze blew from the lake, and the air carried the faint aroma of dried leaves and smoke. Every morning Christine awoke on her porch and stretched, inhaling deeply the soft autumn air that drifted across the city from the countryside beyond.

The third Saturday in October, the day of Rosie's wedding, dawned clear and mild. Christine woke up before seven and lay on her porch listening to the sounds of unusual activity inside the apartment. Even Rosie was up already. Doors banged. Mama's excited voice rose over the sound of running water, followed by Rosie's laughter.

Christine closed her eyes to listen, engraving the sounds in her memory. Tomorrow Rosie would be gone. Christine and Mama would be alone in the apartment. Tonight Rosie would be a wife and would climb aboard the night train to Washington, D.C., on her way to Virginia. Today was the last day Rosie would live with them as a daughter and a sister. The next time she came, she would be a visitor, a wife.

Christine jumped from her mattress and climbed through the window, unmindful of the chilly boards beneath her bare feet. She ran to the kitchen and pushed open the swinging door. Rosie was at the kitchen table sipping a mug of hot coffee. Mama stood at the sink, breaking eggs into a bowl. Both women were smiling, both faces shone in the morning sunshine that broke through the window over the sink in a beam of clear light. How alike they looked with their light hair and heavy-lidded blue eyes, their mouths both curved in laughter.

In a single motion, Christine rounded the table and knelt beside Rosie. She wrapped her arms around Rosie's waist and hugged her tight, feeling the soft heartbeat against her cheek. "I'll miss you, Rosie," she said in a muffled voice against the fabric of Rosie's bathrobe.

Rosie's hand came to rest on the top of her head, one finger gently twirling a strand of hair. "I'll miss you, too. But you'll come to visit as soon as we get settled. And just think of all the marines I'll be able to introduce you to!"

"Now, Roseann," Mama's voice interjected, "you know Christine is much too young to be dating marines. Maybe when she is nineteen like you. Maybe then. But not before. One is still more than enough to worry about."

With a laugh Christine looked up at the two women smiling down at her. Some things never changed.

14

◆ ◆ ◆ ◆ ◆

End of Summer

Christine sat in the chair in front of Tillie's mirror, staring at the face that gazed back at her with wide brown eyes.

"Just look at the difference," Tillie said with satisfaction as she smoothed out the last strand of Christine's hair with a brush. "It's high time you got rid of that braid. Just see what a few curls will do. You're a real lady now, and a right pretty one, too, if I do say so. You'll turn heads for sure."

Christine wasn't sure she agreed with Tillie about turning heads, but she liked the way she looked. She shook her head, missing the weight of the braid swinging across her back. The braid was gone, and her face was framed with a soft halo of dark curls. But Tillie was right about her looking older. She looked like a real bridesmaid now.

"Tell your mom and Rosie to hurry down," Tillie

said, untying the cape draped around Christine's shoulders. "We have to keep the ball rolling. Can't have a bride late for her own wedding."

Two hours later, they left for the church in Uncle Stanislaus's black Packard, which he had washed and polished for the occasion.

The church was already beginning to fill when they arrived for the ceremony. Uncle Stanislaus stood at the back with them, waiting for the wedding march to signal the moment when he would escort Rosie down the aisle. Christine could see Arlene sitting on the aisle near the front. Arlene had said she was going to be the first one at the church to get the best seat, and Christine could see she had been as good as her word. Aunt Sophie was seated beside Mrs. Himmelstein, who had taken a cab over with the Fazios and who insisted that she wouldn't have missed this day if she had been laid up with two broken legs.

Across the aisle sat the O'Malleys, who had traveled all the way from Cedar Rapids. Their family alone filled four pews. The night before Mr. O'Malley had taken them all out to dinner after the rehearsal. It was clear the O'Malleys loved Rosie at first sight, and that made Mama happy.

Chris O'Malley had a cousin George who was fourteen and who had started high school that fall. His ears stuck out like wings from the side of his head, but he was funny and didn't seem to mind that Christine was only in seventh grade. She craned her neck until she saw where he was sitting in the third pew. At the last minute, Tillie rushed in, puffing and blowing from having to hurry, and sat beside the Bertacchis and the Chins.

At the back of the church, Mama kissed Rosie and held her tight. "Be happy, child," Christine heard her say softly. "If only your father were here. . . ." She let the sentence drift away and turned to walk down the aisle to her place in the front pew. It was the first any of them had mentioned Papa that day. Christine closed her eyes, praying that by the time she got married Papa would be home to take her down the aisle. Papa would bend down to kiss her, tell her how beautiful she looked and that he hoped she would be happy.

The familiar opening four notes of "Here Comes the Bride" pumped from the pipe organ overhead in the choir loft. At the far end of the aisle, in front of the altar, Chris O'Malley moved into place to wait for Rosie. Christine turned to look at her sister, smiling and radiant, as she took the arm offered by Uncle Stanislaus. Taking a deep breath, Christine began the slow march down the aisle.

After the long ceremony, they all walked the two blocks to the Veterans of Foreign Wars Hall on Broadway. Christine walked beside Arlene, who for once was almost speechless. She seemed to be awed by the crowd of people and the sight of Christine, who, she whispered, looked very grown-up in her blue velvet dress and her curled hair.

At the hall, there was lots of potato salad, pierogi, sausage, and cabbage slaw as well as shimmering molds of Jell-O. There was plenty of wine, too, and a jukebox with all the latest songs.

Christine danced with Uncle Stanislaus, Mr. Fazio, and Chris's cousin George, who didn't seem to notice that she stepped on his feet. She tried to get Mr. Chin to do the polka, but he just laughed and said she couldn't teach an old dog a new trick. So she and Arlene danced the polka around the room until they were both breathless and glowed from perspiration. But this time they were careful to stay on their feet at the end.

Late in the day, when the hall had grown warm from the wine and the dancing, Christine walked down Broadway with George. The breeze was cooler now and carried moisture from the lake. Christine held out her tongue to taste the air. A change in the weather was coming.

George took her hand as they walked along the street, looking into store windows.

"Now that the war's over, I'm going to travel someday," he said when they stood in front of a travel agency with a window full of posters. "I'm going to be an engineer and go all over the world."

"If Papa comes home, I'd like to travel, too. But I couldn't leave Mama by herself." Christine looked down at the sidewalk. It was the first time she had ever expressed the thought *if* to anyone but Aunt Sophie.

"Where is your dad?"

"We don't know. Maybe somewhere in Poland. Mama, Rosie, and I came over right before the war started, but he couldn't come then. He stayed in Poland. We never heard. . . ." She let her voice trail off. There was really nothing more to explain.

"Gee, that's tough."

In silence they turned and headed back to the VFW hall. The sun was setting. One by one the lights of the city flickered on, transforming the grimy buildings into places of wonder and discovery.

"Some day I'd like to live in Chicago," George said, echoing her thoughts. "I really like it here."

He pulled her to a stop in the shadow of a deserted stoop. She felt his hand on her shoulder as he leaned toward her, their bodies touching only for a moment before he kissed her, half on her lips, half on her cheek. His lips pressed lightly. They were soft and tasted of wine and spice. Christine closed her eyes, letting the kiss linger, savoring the touch and the taste.

"That's for good-bye," he said, releasing her hand. "I'll write to you, if that's okay."

"I'd like that."

They turned into the doorway of the hall, where they could hear the jukebox playing "Don't Get Around Much Any More."

George held the door for her, and together they entered the room. A short time later, the party ended as Rosie and Chris prepared to leave for the train station.

Just before she changed into a traveling suit, Rosie threw her bouquet. She threw it right at Christine, but even so Christine almost dropped it and blushed as the onlookers laughed and clapped.

The wedding dress was carefully folded into a box and locked in the trunk of the Packard. In a final flurry of farewells, Rosie and Chris said their good-byes to the remaining family members.

Christine tried to swallow the lump in her throat as Rosie put her arms around her. "Come see us soon," she whispered into Christine's ear and kissed her cheek. Christine nodded and squeezed her eyes shut.

When she opened them, Rosie was gone, out of the bright lights of the hall into the darkness, as though the night had suddenly swallowed her.

After the last of the guests had gone, Christine and Mama took a cab together back to Sheffield Avenue. Mama sat silently on the ride home, deep in thought, or perhaps just worn out. Christine felt as tired as the night she had worked at Peavy's, and empty, as though all her emotions had been used up. She leaned her head back against the car seat and let the day's events drift across her mind like newsreel images flickering across the screen. But the one that kept returning was the image of George's face bending toward hers and the touch of his lips on hers.

The cabdriver pulled up to the curb. Mama handed him seventy-five cents, and the cab pulled away. It wasn't until Christine and Mama started up the stoop that they saw the man standing on the top step, silhouetted against the front of the building.

"Mrs. Kosinski?" he said in a heavy accent as they approached.

"I am Mrs. Kosinski. You are looking for me?" Mama's voice was soft, the words spoken slowly.

"Mrs. Józef Kosinski?"

"Yes. Do I know you?"

"I am coming from your sister-in-law's house. A neighbor tells me where you live. She says you have a wedding. So I come and wait."

"You look for me?"

"I am bringing news."

On the bottom step, Christine stood motionless, her hand gripping the iron rail.

The man stepped forward out of the shadows and clasped Mama's hands. "I have news. Józef, he is alive."

With a cry, Mama sank down onto the step. "Oh, my God, is this true? Are you saying the truth?"

The man stood above her. He answered in Polish, and Christine listened hard to follow the words. "I have seen him. He is very ill, but he is alive and is getting better. I was with him at Dachau. I was with him when they freed us."

Christine closed her eyes and clung to the rail. Papa was alive. The news made her head spin, her heart stop. And yet what this man was saying didn't surprise her. She had felt it all along, had known in her bones that Papa could not be dead. But now they *knew*, really knew, and the wondering, the wishing were over. It was as though for six years their lives had stopped, and now at last they could get on with them again.

"You know him? You know Józef?" Mama's voice sounded small. Her head bent into her hands. The man sat beside her.

"Yes. But for many months I did not know he was alive. We were all starving, close to death. I was very ill myself, but Józef . . ." He shook his head slowly. "Józef was unconscious, in a semicoma for a long time, and it wasn't until I began to get better and discovered he was still alive that I could tell them . . ." He began to cough and Mama jumped up beside him.

"Come. We go inside. I am forgetting myself. I am forgetting all except Józef is alive. Come. I make you a cup of tea and you tell me all."

By the time Mama had made a pot of tea and the three of them were sitting around the kitchen table, Christine had learned that the man's name was Steven Kaczmarek and he had arrived in Chicago only that day on his way to live with relatives in Saint Louis. Both he and Mama spoke in Polish very fast, and Christine had to wait until after he left to be sure she had not missed any of the story of Steven Kaczmarek and Papa: how both of them had been sent to Dachau by the Nazis as political prisoners, how they had both survived only by some miracle and by the grace of a merciful God, how Papa was still too sick to travel but was at last out of danger.

Papa had written them a letter, which Steven Kaczmarek had given to Mama. It was brief and the handwriting was shaky, but Papa had written it himself. It stated that he had never stopped thinking of them, that it was thoughts of them that had kept him alive, and that he hoped to be with them by Christmas.

By Christmas. That was not so long, Christine thought. She would never forget this day. Rosie's wedding and news of Papa coming home. What a wedding present this news would be for Rosie tomorrow. If only they had known it before she left.

"I must go to him," Mama had said in English after reading the letter. "I must go at once."

"No," Steven had said, shaking his head. "He knew you would say this. Poland is no place to go now. Everything is torn apart. Everywhere there is destruction and hunger. He will rest easier knowing you are here. He said, 'Tell her it is better to be there when I come. She should not come to Poland now.'"

"Well, we shall see," was all Mama had said, but Christine knew she would think more about it.

After Mr. Kaczmarek had left to spend the night with a friend, Mama sank onto the old worn sofa in the living room and pulled Christine down beside her. Mama's eyes filled with tears as she wrapped her arms around Christine, rocking back and forth with her as though cradling a child. For a moment Christine felt herself back in Kraków on the swing beneath the old apple tree. But that was in the past, and now she could let the past go.

"Oh, Christine," Mama crooned, "if you knew, if you only knew . . ."

Christine felt Mama's tears warm on her cheek. Her own eyes filled, the tears overflowing, running with Mama's down both their cheeks.

"We must get some sleep, *troche* Christine," Mama said at last, drying her eyes. "So much is happening, I think it is all a dream. Tomorrow we will sort everything out. We will think about it all then. Tonight we can dream about Papa being alive."

Christine waited until Mama had closed her bedroom door. Then she undressed and turned out the lights. No need tonight to leave one on for Rosie. She would never again awaken to see Rosie dancing with a sailor to the music of a record on the old Victrola.

She climbed out onto the porch, closing the window behind her. The streets were silent. By this hour even the Saturday-night crowds had faded away. She lay down on her mattress and pulled the blanket up to her chin. Across the street she could see the billboard with the ship sinking into the water. No more would she have to dream about Papa on that sinking ship or rowing across the ocean in a dinghy to the shores of Chicago. Tonight she could dream about Papa arriving on their doorstep, thinner perhaps, and frail, but still Papa. Tonight she would dream of the day he'd come home.

She closed her eyes, welcoming the dream. But before the first picture of Papa could form in her mind, she fell into deep, dreamless sleep.

Early in the morning Christine awoke before sunrise. The winds had shifted and blew from the north. Winter was coming on. She shivered and pulled the blanket closer around her. An unexpected quiet hung over the city. Below, only a prowling cat nudged the garbage cans underneath the stoop. Silence had settled on Sheffield Avenue and on the whole world, it seemed.

She lay in the silence thinking about the changes in her life since the beginning of summer: how the war was finally over and the baseball season, too; how Rosie was married and so quickly gone from their lives; how Papa would be coming home, but she would never again be the little girl who sat in his lap.

She thought about her night as a soda jerk and the

banana split lying on the floor at her feet. Now she could even smile about it. She was saving Mr. Peavy's two dollars to buy a Christmas present for Mama. Only now it would be a present for Mama and Papa, something they could enjoy together.

In the stillness of early morning, she let her mind drift to the sailor at the Aragon Ballroom, the feel of his hand pressed against her back, his cheek against her cheek. And finally, as her thoughts shifted to George and the softness of his lips as they touched hers, she felt a tingle run up her spine and closed her eyes to enjoy it.

She listened for the rattle of the El or the rumble of the streetcar on Clark Street, but at that hour, even those sounds had stilled. Now even the Aragon Ballroom would be silent. The musicians would have put away their instruments and started home. The last dance had ended. Summer was over.

In the cold air and hush of early dawn, Christine rose and crawled back through the window, pulling the mattress and blanket in behind her. Quietly lowering the window, she turned the latch to lock it in place and made her way into the bedroom she had shared with Rosie during the winter months. The scent of Rosie's powder and Evening in Paris perfume still hung in the air.

Christine pulled back the flowered spread that covered Rosie's bed. Outside the sky was beginning to brighten. In just a few hours, Arlene would be standing on the stoop, calling, "Hey, Tina! Whatchawanna do today?"

Christine slid under the covers and closed her eyes against the morning light. Pressing her face into the pillow, she inhaled deeply the fragrance of a summer garden.